HEIRS AND PARENTS

HEIRS AND PARENTS

Ralph McInerny

St. Martin's Minotaur
New York

For Russ and Mary Hittinger

www.stmartins.com

Library of Congress Cataloging-in-Publication Data

McInerny, Ralph M.
    Heirs and parents / Ralph McInerny—1st ed.
        p. cm.
      ISBN 0-312-20311-X
      1. Broom, Andrew (Fictitious character)—Fiction. 2. Indiana—Fiction.
    I. Title.

PS3563.A31166 H43 2000
813'.54—dc21

00-025473

First Edition: June 2000

10   9   8   7   6   5   4   3   2   1

HEIRS AND PARENTS

Overlook Cemetery was on the north side of Wyler, at a point where the first explorers of the region had signed a treaty with the indigenous population in which each side sought to best the other. And had. The Indians got firearms and firewater while the French were given permission to settle on the point overlooking the river. It was cool and shady in summer, but infested with mosquitoes and other pesky insects, and after the leaves fell and winter came it was exposed to the winds that gathered momentum as they swept unimpeded across the prairie.

The settlers buried their dead there too, of course, and over time, as the town moved southward and westward, it retained only its role as cemetery.

It was in Overlook, on a cool morning in July, that the body was found.

"What's that car doing out in the Resurrection section?" Will Foley demanded when he pulled up to the maintenance shed at seven-fifteen.

"What car?"

"Over in Resurrection."

This was a part of the cemetery that went way back. There were stones in there with dates you wouldn't believe, graves so old there was nobody to remember who was in them anymore. It was Foley's favorite spot. Drive out there and park, spray the cab with bug juice, and light up. You could imagine those Frenchmen struggling up the bank—wearing armor, if you believed the mural in the post office. Sometimes he ate his lunch out there. Last summer when he hired Helga to mow and water he got her to come along a couple of times. She was scared of him at first. She was scared of lots of things. Of the walkers and joggers, of the relatives who came and haunted graves.

"I can't believe those little plastic signs, Will."

"Which ones?"

"Mom. Dad. Spelled out in pink-and-white plastic flowers."

Foley kind of liked those. It was the goddam walkers and joggers he couldn't stand. Huffing and puffing along with bright eyes and sweatbands, where the hell did they think they were going? "They're running away from death in the cemetery," Helga had said, and then looked oddly at him when he took it for a joke. The walkers swung their arms like soldiers on parade. But parked cars were a special annoyance.

"Probably some walker's car," Rusconi said that July morning.

Parked and then got out to walk? It happened. But Foley couldn't remember a car parked in Resurrection before. The roads were unpaved gravel, it wasn't the best-kept-up part of Overlook, and if you didn't bring protection you were eaten up by mosquitoes.

"Close the window," he had advised Helga when she got tired of waving them away.

"And smell that spray?"

"You're pretty hard to please."

She had thick ropey hair that had started out golden but during the course of the summer got sun-streaked. The first time Foley realized he had parked just to stare at her bouncing along on that mower, he laughed it off, but within a week his workday consisted of finding opportunities to watch Helga, talk to Helga, show off for Helga. He acted like a goddam teenager.

"How long have you worked here?" she asked him.

"Since high school."

Her mouth dropped. "That long?"

"Hey, I'm not that old."

Not to himself, maybe, but he had a dozen years on her, or more. She had finished two years at IU and couldn't wait to get back to Bloomington when summer was over. Her face was freckled from the sun and there was a little mustache of sweat on her upper lip. Her lower lip rolled outward, and she had a habit of running the pink tip of her tongue along it.

"How long you been married?" she asked.

"Since my wedding day."

"Got any kids?"

"Why do you think I got married?"

"You mean you had to?"

"Hey, that's pretty personal." But he said it in a way that encouraged any interest she might have in Will Foley the man.

"Why do you go on working here?"

"At Overlook? I have so many people under me."

"I'm serious. This job doesn't use a fraction of your mind."

He had imagined that it was his build she would notice. He was in great shape, and not from jogging or any other stupid exercise. It was just the way he was. He had twisted his knee in his final season of high school football and that summer taken the job at Overlook, doing what he had hired Helga to do. Mow. Check the sprinklers.

"What do you think about when you're on the mower?" he asked her.

She turned and studied him for a while. She nodded. She knew what he meant. This job, you're by yourself all day, so what do you do? You think. Those headstones and the historical plaque had gotten Foley interested in local history. If anyone ever asked him, he could tell them all about it: the first years; the spanning of the river with a bridge that replaced the ferry that had plied between the two banks; the big influx of immigrants at the turn of the century, which was when the Foleys came. Of course, no one ever asked him and he never brought it up. Fiona couldn't care less about the history of Wyler, Indiana. She had it in her head that they would move to California someday. Or Florida.

"There are cemeteries everywhere," she explained.

They might all seem alike to her, but Overlook was not just another cemetery to Will Foley. He supposed that someday he would be buried there himself. Fiona too, only she got mad as hell at any mention of death. She actually put her hands over her ears. She didn't want to know about any part of his job.

"Want me to go check on that car?" Rusconi said.

"What for?"

"You brought it up." Miffed, Rusconi started his machine and maneuvered it out the gate of the maintenance area, off to dig a grave. Clarence, this summer's college student, had hair as long as Helga's, worn in a ponytail. Foley didn't want to know what his earring meant, if anything.

He went into the office, where Gladys peered over the counter at him as if she were hiding. She pushed a worksheet toward him. She worked for Junius Schmucker, who had inherited Overlook and left it to inertia and his employees to run the place. Gladys had been in Foley's class at Wyler High and had worked here almost as long as he had. She had stopped asking about Fiona. Fiona was married and had the kids, but here was Gladys just where she had been ever since high school. Rusconi tried to make a move on her, but he should have taken a shower first. Foley didn't even want to think how lonely life must be for Gladys.

"The funeral procession should get here about ten-fifteen."

"Rusconi's out digging the grave now."

"He should have done that yesterday."

"In the rain?"

She shrugged. It never rained in the office.

"Gladys, did you notice that car parked out in Resurrection?"

She forgot to keep her mouth shut so her teeth wouldn't hang out. "When?"

"This morning."

She inhaled and rolled her eyes. Maybe she was right. Lovers found the cemetery an aphrodisiac. Maybe they had fallen asleep and been there all night. He hadn't thought of that. It seemed an extra reason to check it out.

As he drove up the road and parked behind the car he couldn't see anyone in it, but the trees reflecting off the windows made them opaque. He slammed his door when he got out and ground his feet in the gravel as he approached but no head, or heads, popped into view. The sunroof was open and so was the window on the driver's side. The girl lay across the front seat. Blood from the gaping wound in her throat had flowed into the ropey blond hair that hung to the floor. The blue eyes stared dully through the sunroof.

It was Helga.

2

"A body in the cemetery? No kidding."

Alex Hollister made a face but he wanted to laugh. When he was a kid they would call up the drugstore and ask if they had Prince Albert in the can. They did? Well, don't flush it. Alex was the constable of Wyler, which was the county seat and therefore protected, patrolled, and policed by the sheriff. Exactly what the role of constable was supposed to be in these circumstances was a matter of debate from time to time, whenever the city budget was scrutinized by reformers. But Alex had been constable since returning from the war. *The war.* He had been part of the American occupation forces in Italy and had been aide-de-camp of a young lawyer who had been put in charge of Agrigento. They had about as much control over that Sicilian city as Alex was to have over Wyler. Phone calls like this one were not uncommon.

"I will leave no stone unturned," he answered, watching the small color tv set he had going on his desk. It was inaudible but he just liked to watch that perky little girl with the wide smile. Every morning she was the same, bright, bouncy, interested, and cute as a button.

"Alex, this is Will Foley, I work at Overlook. There is a parked vehicle out here with a dead body in it. A woman. She's been killed."

"Willis Foley?"

"Yes."

"Played tight end for Wyler High?"

"That's right."

"You're working at Overlook?"

"I've been here since high school."

"Why didn't you play college ball?"

"My knee."

Alex remembered, or thought he remembered, something about that. A great career blighted.

"Willis, do me a favor, will you? Call the sheriff. I let him handle things like this."

"But they told me to call you."

"They did!"

"They thought I was kidding."

"Who'd you talk to?"

"I didn't get his name."

Alex sat forward and turned off the television. His Stetson hung on a hook beside the door. He felt vaguely stirred by the thought of checking out this call. If it wasn't a joke, he could sock it to Sheriff Cleary, maybe even let the papers know how incompetent Cleary's office was. Years ago Alex had thought of running for sheriff, but the prospect of giving up his sinecure for real responsibility deterred him. He did wish people appreciated the fact that there had been a constable in Wyler long before there was a sheriff.

"Where are you?"

"At Overlook."

"Where will I find you?"

"In the office."

"Wait for me there."

He hung up the phone. He turned on the television, but there was a commercial going so he had to settle for a memory of that perky, encouraging smile. He eased himself from his chair, straightening his back slowly to get the kinks out of it. He leveled the Stetson across his eyes and opened the door. Should he bring a weapon? He decided to strap on a revolver. Outside, he clamped the light on top of his car and set out. He tried out the siren when he was clear of downtown but he couldn't stand the sound of the thing and turned it off.

It occurred to him that he would have been headed for Overlook in a few hours anyway, to watch them put old Waggoner in the ground. It looked like a nice day for a funeral. Hazy, not too hot.

The office at Overlook was in the Victorian house that had been built just inside the entrance. It had been designed as a residence for the manager as well as administrative offices, but no man with a family would live in it, so it had the look of a haunted house. Its upstairs windows stared vacantly at the world, there was a lot of gingerbread woodwork, and a huge L-shaped porch wrapped around the house. Will Foley came out the door and down to the car and identified himself. He seemed disappointed at the nonofficial vehicle and the make-shift light. Alex half wished he'd driven in with the siren on.

"I'll go first, in the pickup."

"I'll follow you," Alex said gruffly. A seventy-five-year-old constable was not an imposing sight, he knew that, but by keeping out of harm's way he warded off embarrassing questions. Not that he thought anyone could get him fired. A question had once been raised about his age at a council meeting and brought on outraged charges of ageism. Apparently it was now unconstitutional to notice that age takes a lot out of a man.

Foley climbed into his pickup and a little puff of black smoke came out of his exhaust when he started down the road. Alex kept his own car in top-notch condition. It was twenty years old, had 98,000 miles on it, burned no oil, but made up for it in gas. He loved it. These gravelly roads spit up stones, and he kept a distance from the pickup, not wanting any nicks.

It had been a while since he had been to Overlook but it might have been yesterday, the place was so familiar. They had played here as kids, getting shagged away by the caretaker and sliding down the banks to the river. Did kids still play along the river, fish, canoe, camp out nights? Everything was too organized now.

Foley still looked like a football player and there didn't seem to be anything wrong with his knee when he came to a stop and hopped out of the pickup, waiting for Alex to come up before he started toward the vehicle. It was parked in the shade, but little patches of sun jumped around on it, coming through the moving branches above. Alex stared in at the woman.

"Someone cut her throat."

Foley stood there, waiting. Alex wished he had brought the phone from his car. He tipped the Stetson back.

"I think we better call the sheriff."

"I told you what they said."

"I'll call." He started toward his car, then turned. "And I'll call Andrew Broom too."

3

"Who was it, Andrew?"

"Alex Hollister."

Susannah turned from her mirror. He had tried to sound matter-of-fact, but Susannah had a wife's radar and detected something.

"A girl had her throat slit in Overlook Cemetery."

"My God! Why did he call you?"

"He already called the sheriff."

"Who was the girl?"

He crossed to her and took her hand when he said it. "Helga Bjornsen."

Silence. Susannah's eyes searching his. The rustle of their thoughts was almost audible. But then Susannah put her hand over his.

"I don't think Alex knew she was working in the office this summer, Susannah. That isn't why he called. He wants me to check it out to make sure the sheriff takes him seriously."

"About a murder?" Then, as if realizing that they were talking about the violent death of someone they had both known, Susannah shuddered.

"I told Alex I'd call Cleary."

The sheriff was still at his office, which made Alex's worry seem well founded.

"Andrew, we are providing escort for the funeral procession. I will go to Overlook after that. I told Alex to keep his shirt on and in a couple hours—"

"Send someone else."

"Like who?"

"You can't have a murder reported and just put off looking into it."

"Andrew, it was *Alex* who called. Constable Alex Hollister. Now, just what the hell is he doing in Overlook Cemetery at this hour of the morning finding dead bodies?" Cleary stopped to guffaw. "Dead bodies in the cemetery, Andrew. And you want me to rush right out there?"

"Deputize me and I'll go."

"Aren't you going to the funeral?"

"It doesn't start until ten. Maurice, I'll meet you at Overlook."

The sheriff was still complaining when Andrew hung up. Alex might be a bit of a joke as constable, but Maurice Cleary, forever on his dignity, was worse. As for himself, whether Alex or Cleary knew it, he was checking on the death of an employee.

Foster had recommended her when she applied for summer

13

work at the *Dealer* and he had nothing for her. "I felt like inventing a spot for her."

"Oh?"

"Wait till you see her."

She was beautiful with the beauty of youth. It would have been possible to think that she would never age, if it had not been for her eyes. They were watchful eyes, not quite wary, as if the world had more surprises than she cared for and she just wasn't sure of Andrew or of his nephew Gerald or of Susannah.

"She should be outside," Gerald had said. "Not cooped up in an office."

Andrew took heart from Gerald's interest in the girl. Was it possible he could be weaned away from his passion for Julie McGough? Andrew could not imagine that beautiful girl with the golden hair dead, and he wore a frown when he drove through the gates at Overlook.

4

The First Presbyterian Church of Wyler was packed. Ushers had wedged as many as they could into each pew; they had allowed some to mount to the choir loft, much to the alarm of Mrs. Sharp, the organist; mourners were standing along the walls. The Reverend Hauerwas sailed down the aisle with his robe flying and gave instructions that folding chairs were to be brought in from the social center. Clearly, the late Stanley Waggoner was going to be sent on his way with all the pomp and circumstance that the town could muster.

And rightly so. Stanley, who allegedly had been gaga for five years, was the last of the Waggoner family that had brought Wyler into the twentieth century. The manufacture of automobiles had once been a cottage industry and half a dozen towns in Indiana produced them—the Auburn, the Stu-

debaker, the Waggoner. Until the Second World War a stream
of shiny, sturdy vehicles had issued from the Waggoner plant
on the west side of town and putted across the nation. When
war was declared, getting a government contract to manufacture military vehicles was the key to survival. Waggoner of
Wyler had landed no such contracts. For four years, no automobiles were produced. The bulk of the workforce went off
to battle. The rationing of gasoline made the carefree days of
prewar motoring seem a casualty of fascism. Stanley's father,
the ineffable Clement, had decided to put the great capacity
of the plant to work producing the kind of cheap novelties
once supplied by Japan to Crackerjacks and the like. On this
diminished basis, a muted hum continued to issue from the
plant until V-J Day. Victory in the Pacific confirmed the defeat
of Waggoner of Wyler.

Theories abounded as to what exactly had gone wrong.
Sociologists thought they understood it; historians spoke know-
ingly of demographic shifts; economists produced charts and
graphs. But all these explanations were tautologous. Waggoner
Motors had failed because Waggoner Motors had failed. Simpler theories were favored in such watering holes as the Round
Ball Lounge.

"Clem Waggoner was a dumb son of a bitch."

Heads nodded in agreement. But ignorance needs a context
in which to flourish. Clem's father had simply done what his
father had done before him, and Schuyler Waggoner had prospered and Wyler with him. Without the war, Clem's inepti-
tude would never have been revealed. After the war, veterans
returned to Wyler, but many of them moved on—to South
Bend, to Detroit. But the role of the Waggoners in Wyler
was not exhausted. Stanley endeared himself to the town in a

way that none of his forebears had. He became a philanthropist.

"We have been spared the ravages of industrialization," he said in a speech dedicating the new library he had given the town. And at the high school commencement, alluding to the new athletic fields he had provided, he remarked that runners and jumpers could gulp down the unsullied Indiana air as they ran down the cinder tracks to glory. The demise of the family business was, for Stanley, a mark of favor on the part of the Presbyterian deity. Stanley had been the principal benefactor in the building of this magnificent edifice from which his mortal remains would be taken to Overlook Cemetery.

Hauerwas had already begun his eulogy when Andrew got there. He spotted Susannah's picture hat way down front.

"Do you want to join Mrs. Broom?" an usher whispered in his ear. Andrew turned. It was Phillips, a dentist with offices in the Hoosier Towers.

"Will there be a pause?"

"In a sermon?"

"I better wait."

"When he's through, it's over."

Reluctantly, Andrew followed Phillips down the aisle, aware of the curious, annoyed looks that accompanied their progress. Andrew kept his eyes fixed on Phillips's back, not wanting to encounter the eyes of the preacher, whose tone seemed to be commenting on this interruption. It was a relief to slide in beside Susannah. Phillips stood beside the pew, as if to make sure Andrew got seated. Finally he left. Susannah's hand closed over Andrew's.

It was not true that the end of the sermon signaled the end of the service. After Hauerwas's peroration, in which he summarized his effort to show that the gospel teaching that the rich will find it hard to enter heaven was not applicable in the case of the deceased, a stream of people went to the pulpit and expressed their grief at the passing of Stanley Waggoner. One of them had been his secretary a quarter of a century before. It seemed that Stanley's smile had been radiant and his manner always warm but proper, and it had been a joy to take dictation from him.

"He left her ten thousand," a voice whispered from behind.

Distant cousins, similarly moved by hints about bequests, expressed regret at their inability to visit Stanley when he was alive but felt honored to be here now.

Stanley's investments in foreign stock, particularly Japanese automobiles, had replenished the family fortune, and Frank McGough's discovery of some forgotten holdings from the first quarter of the century had established Stanley as a veritable Croesus. McGough, Andrew's major rival in Wyler, sat with the family and comported himself as if he and God were good friends. Andrew felt a twinge of regret that his rival had gotten the Waggoner business. It had not seemed much of a plum at the time he himself might have represented the family. It was a great relief that McGough did not take his turn in the pulpit.

There was a motorcycle escort to halt traffic so that the funeral cortege could proceed without interruption to Overlook Cemetery. Pedestrians stopped and stared; people came out of their houses and watched the long line of cars go by. Baffle himself drove the hearse and never exceeded twenty miles per hour. It was an odd thought that solemnity is a matter of speed.

"Did you notice the youngish woman, beautiful in black, who wasn't allowed to speak?" Susannah asked.

"I wonder who she was."

"She claims to be Stanley's wife."

"A whacko?"

"Julie didn't say."

"Julie!"

"I thought she would know."

Julie was a lovely girl whose single but sufficient flaw was that she was Frank McGough's daughter. A woman showing up at this point and claiming to be married to Frank McGough's enormously wealthy client would have sown some concern in the lawyer's office.

They were nearing the entrance to Overlook, and the whole aspect of the place was different from an hour or so before when Andrew had come in response to Alex Hollister's request. Peace seemed to sit softly on the mown lawns, the irregular rows of markers might have been counting off man's allotted span, and there were flowers everywhere. Death seemed an idea, an abstraction, something as hidden as the lifeless body of Stanley Waggoner was hidden in the ornate and expensive coffin that was eased onto the device that eventually would lower it into the ground. But even the hole that would receive it was camouflaged by edgings of artificial grass. A canopy had been set up over the scene and the Reverend Hauerwas was ready to do his thing once more. What a contrast to the stark reality of the murdered girl in the car parked at the far end of the cemetery.

5

As secretary of Junius Schmucker, the proprietor and sexton of Overlook Cemetery, Gladys Winter was not in an ideal spot to meet the man of her dreams. Will Foley was the closest there was to a social equal among the grounds and maintenance crew but Gladys knew or suspected too much about him to really respect him anymore. Schmucker himself? He was married and he was fat; when he wasn't off on one of his unscheduled trips, he spent most of the day in his office sitting at his computer, checking sites on the Internet he obviously did not want Gladys to see when she went in there. He was nervous as a cat until he could bring something else up on the screen. Not that it was necessary. The angle Gladys had when she entered the office made his computer screen unreadable by her. There was a large window between this office and hers but the blinds were always closed, making it more of a wall than the wall itself.

Schmucker had inherited the cemetery. Actually two cemeteries, Overlook and Oak Lawn, over in Jenkins. But Oak Lawn was all sold out and needed little looking after. Three men were sent over there for a half day once a week, and that was about it. Most of the complaints they received were from people who had someone buried at Oak Lawn.

"I had to wade through knee-high grass to get to the grave and if I hadn't known where it was I'd never have found it."

"A crew was out there yesterday," Gladys would answer patiently. The families of the deceased were, after the first week or two of mourning, a pain in the whatchamacallit, in Gladys's experience.

"Doing what?"

"Mowing. Tending the graves."

"Humph. Well, I mowed around Orville's grave myself."

Junius Schmucker thought she was being too patient. Away from his computer, he actually seemed to notice her, and Gladys tried to convince herself he wasn't all that bad-looking. Weight can be taken off and maybe with contact lenses . . . He seemed to be trying to peer down her blouse. She turned away, slowly.

"How is Gloria?"

It was a bore, reminding men that they had wives. Suddenly it seemed that every man she knew was married. She just did not understand how she had been passed by, and neither did her married friend Regina, who was always proposing desperate remedies. They had chipped in and run an ad on local television: "SWF, fun loving, likes picnics, line dancing and walks in the woods. Are you ready to turn over a new leaf?

Give me a call." The response was immediate. Regina agreed to check out one respondent while Gladys waited in the car outside the bar; the doors of the car were locked and she wore a large billed cap pulled low over her eyes. A good thing. Junius Schmucker walked within a foot of the car and didn't notice her. She sighed with relief when he went into the bar. Ten minutes later, Regina came out, piled into the passenger seat, and told Gladys to drive. Then she burst out laughing.

"What happened?"

"Nothing!"

"Wasn't he there?"

"I don't know. But I wouldn't want you going with any man who was."

That was the end of that great experiment. She and Regina went line dancing, but that only created the impression of being on a date. Men danced with them, which was fine, but it was also the end of it. Nonetheless, she was forever grateful to Regina for taking such trouble on her behalf.

Gladys hated everything about funerals. She hated to see the crew go off to dig the grave and get things ready; she hated it when the funeral procession came through the gates and wound off along one of the narrow paved roads. She hated them because they had stopped meaning anything to her anymore. At first she had watched wide-eyed and openmouthed from the office, her gaze fixed on the hearse bearing the body that soon would be put into the ground for all eternity. Suddenly life seemed the saddest thing in the world, a few years of delusion while we refuse to think of the fact that we must die and then, bingo, it's all over and another procession was coming through the gates. Death and burial seemed the goal of life, as if everyone was on a long aimless journey that must eventually end here. Junius Schmucker just stared at her when she tried to express her feelings.

"It's a dirty business, but someone has to do it."

"It's so sad."

"You had a choice. I inherited this job."

This was before Junius put in the very powerful and expensive computer that enabled him to while away the day in the sexton's office.

"It could be worse."

"What do you mean?"

"How would you like to be an undertaker?"

She didn't even want to think about it. But Junius was right. They never confronted the reality of death. Bodies came to them already in boxes; when they were buried they were immediately covered up and buried again under heaps of flowers. That was why finding Helga's body in the car parked way out in Resurrection had been such a shock.

Gladys took Junius's golf cart out to the scene, not knowing how much she wanted to see.

"Woman with her throat slit," Rusconi had told her.

Why hadn't he said it was Helga? Maybe he hadn't known. Maybe he didn't recognize her, although that seemed unlikely. Helga had made last summer a torture for Gladys. Suddenly the place was electric with sexual signals, every man there acting and talking differently because Helga was on the crew. It made some of them gentler, it made some of them swagger, it reduced Will Foley to watchful silence.

"She should cut her hair," Gladys said once when she came outside and saw Will watching the single long braid of Helga's hair bounce off her backside as she drove her little tractor onto the road. "It could get caught in something."

23

Will pretended he hadn't been watching her. Ha. Why wasn't there some way to get him to look at her the way he looked at Helga? She told herself why. She was a dozen years older than Helga, she had known Will and Fiona forever, she was part of the furniture around here, and her hair wouldn't have grown that long if she never cut it again.

When she arrived out at Resurrection in the golf cart, there were two sheriff patrol cars, as well as another car with a light on top. A 911 emergency ambulance came tearing over the winding road with its siren wailing and Gladys went to stand next to Will Foley, who was off to the side.

"What happened?"

He looked at her. "There's a dead woman." There was something in his eyes as he said it and she looked again. The car was just like Will Foley's. "Helga," he added.

"Helga!" Gladys just drifted toward the car, passing among the uniformed deputies to the open driver's door, and looked in at the body sprawled across the front seat. It took a moment before she realized what was wrong with the throat but it was the hair that caught and held her attention. Golden, thick, matted with blood now, but still a glorious sight.

When she went back to where she had left Will Foley, he was no longer there.

6

One look at the murder scene and Cleary was on the phone to Indianapolis and the IBI. His department was not equipped to handle anything like this and it was routine for him to bring in the state bureau of investigation when anything requiring technical and scientific gathering and assessment of evidence came up. This happened regularly but not, thank God, frequently.

"I'll have the lab unit from Jasper over there in twenty minutes," Hanson said. "Want me there?"

Cleary winced at the mention of Jasper. Wyler was a town of over fifty thousand inhabitants, as large as Jasper, but Wyler and its county were almost coterminous, whereas Jasper was the seat of a county that stretched along the Illinois border for miles and miles, encompassing all kinds of taxable property and enterprises. It had all the latest things in crime investigation.

"Can you come?" he asked Hanson.

"Not before this afternoon."

Cleary had a deputy wait at the murder scene to welcome the crew from Jasper. There were some things a man cannot bear. Besides, he had to get downtown to the Waggoner funeral. He pulled every other patrol car out of the cemetery, needing them for escort. The Wyler paramedics had managed to ascertain that the dead girl was dead and were more than willing to leave everything untouched until the Jasper unit arrived.

At the church, before going inside, Cleary called his office to let them know where he was and what was happening.

"Greene just left here, mad as a hornet."

Cleary groaned. Greene was the coroner. Apparently 911 had contacted him and he resented this delayed notification of a death in his jurisdiction. Greene rightly suspected that he was a figure of fun or an object of disdain to those around him and this increased his pomposity in self-defense. He went through life with the sense of being slighted and underestimated. He would make a nuisance of himself over the murder of that girl.

It was almost a relief to settle down at the funeral service for Stanley Waggoner. The deceased had lived a long and useless life, redeeming his unearned wealth by distributing it liberally around the town where his family had prospered. As much as he could, he persuaded the grateful citizens not to name these benefactions after his family, but there was the Waggoner School and Waggoner Park and Waggoner Mall and the Waggoner Museum of Premodern Art.

"Premodern?" visitors would ask.

"Art you can tell what it is."

"Ah."

This made Stanley sound like a stick-in-the-mud. What did it cost him to admire a canvas with one streak of paint on it? His rule was that if he could have done it himself, he didn't want it hanging in the Waggoner museum.

Not that Stanley was a frequent presence. He hadn't lived in Wyler for years and everyone assumed he was out there living it up like the other rich people, so it came as something of a surprise to learn that he had spent his last years in a nursing home in the southern part of the state.

Maurice Cleary got settled in a pew and turned off his hearing aid. He was breathing a littler easier now. Andrew Broom had shamed him into going to the cemetery to look into the death of that girl, and it might have caused him to miss the funeral. But everything was working out all right after all, at least for the living.

Andrew should have shown a little more understanding when Maurice explained that it was Alex Hollister who was reporting the body. But pressing the point might have brought to light the fact that Will Foley had called the sheriff's office first and been deflected to the constable. It wasn't that Foley's report was doubted, but they had their hands full this morning with Stanley Waggoner's funeral. Anyway, things were under control now. A medical examiner team on its way from Jasper. Hanson on his way from Indianapolis. Maurice felt like a general practitioner who turned anything difficult over to the specialists.

Andrew and the missus were sitting shoulder to shoulder, close as teenagers. Maurice tried to remember the last time he and Jeannette had acted as if their marriage was anything more than an armed truce. Why had Andrew been so willing to go out to Overlook to check out the report of a body? Any other lawyer, Maurice might have thought he was drumming up business, but Andrew's problem was how to turn down requests for representation without getting a reputation for being too big for his britches.

Andrew had known the girl's name. Helga Bjornsen. What a way to go. With the sermon as background noise, Maurice imagined what had gone on in that parked car out at Overview. Rape? A lovers' quarrel? But the slit throat seemed too violent for either of those. Strangling would have been enough. He closed his eyes and thought of the dead girl lying on the front seat of the car, her long golden hair stained with the blood that had poured from that awful wound.

Whoever did that was going to pay the price, or his name wasn't Maurice Cleary. Of course, it would be up to Hanson to identify the killer, but when he did, Maurice personally would make the arrest.

7

Gerald Rowan was relieved when his uncle Andrew said he need not attend the funeral of Stanley Waggoner. "Susannah and I will show the flag, Gerald."

"The passing of an era," Gerald murmured, and Andrew looked at him.

"Stanley was pushing eighty and almost no one knew him personally. There was more emotion involved when Waggoner stopped making cars."

Without Susannah in the office, Gerald's secretary, Bernice, would manage the phones, leaving Gerald with several unimpeded hours to prepare briefs for the personal injury case he was working on. But with his door closed and the realization that he was all alone in the office, he found himself unable to concentrate. He put on a CD, Mozart sonatas, a recommendation of Julie's.

"It will shape your emotions," she said, and he admired the shape of her lips as she said this. "It will put them at the service of your mind."

They were clinging to one another at the time, parked up the street from the imposing McGough home, not wanting to be noticed by her father. Their situation rivaled that of Romeo and Juliet. Frank McGough was adamantly opposed to his daughter's having anything to do with the nephew and partner of his arch rival, Andrew Broom. Andrew, in turn, questioned Gerald's good sense in being attracted to Julie.

"Andrew, she's beautiful."

"So was her mother."

"Well."

"She is Frank McGough's daughter. The man should have been disbarred years ago. He's scarcely better than a crook."

Exaggerations, Susannah explained. Andrew had bested Frank McGough in every head-on encounter, but that had not prevented McGough from flourishing in other matters. Once the *Dealer* had described Frank McGough as the leading lawyer of Wyler and Andrew had been beside himself.

"Tell Foster," Susannah said.

"I will not demean myself. Any editor who would print such nonsense is beyond the reach of reason."

Only Susannah, and to some extent Gerald, knew how betrayed Andrew had felt. The *Dealer* was a client of Andrew's. A week after the offending story, Foster called the office about a threatened libel suit. Someone had been mistakenly identified as male rather than female in an obituary and the family was bringing suit.

"That's nonsense," Andrew said. "Who's their lawyer?"

"Frank McGough."

"The leading lawyer of Wyler? Oh, you are in trouble, Foster."

"What do you mean, leading lawyer?"

"I quote the *Dealer*."

Foster checked and found the offending sentence. "Andrew, the reporter was quoting a client of McGough's."

"Then why wasn't the remark in quotes?"

"My God, Andrew, it's not as if we had called you a woman."

The rancor dissolved in laughter. Andrew visited the bereaved family who had taken offense at the gender change attributed to their loved one, offered apologies and the covering of funeral expenses by the *Dealer*.

The main effect of Mozart on Gerald was to keep his mind on Julie. He turned off the music and Bernice came in and put a message on his desk.

"This is from the answering service. As you can see, she wants to come by immediately after the funeral."

Gerald picked up the note. "Mrs. Stanley Waggoner?"

Bernice shrugged.

"Wasn't Stanley a bachelor?"

"He was the last time I heard."

It seemed an excuse to call Julie. She was breathless when she picked up the phone.

"Mademoiselle Pouffante?" He said this in the fruity French accent that had amused Julie in the past.

"Gerald?" She spoke in a whisper and might have been cupping the phone as well.

"Can you talk?"

"Daddy went on to the cemetery. He let me escape."

"How was it?"

"How does one rank funerals?"

"Was the widow there?"

"The widow?"

"Mrs. Stanley Waggoner. I am reading from a note. Someone calling herself that will be showing up here momentarily."

"Oh, Gerald, she's a fraud. She was a nurse where Stanley spent his last years."

"Sounds romantic."

"If Andrew takes her as a client it will just renew animosities."

"Andrew?"

"Gerald, don't you dare."

"Tonight?"

"There is a talk at St. Benedict's on the Pakistan missions."

"My favorite topic. What time?"

They would meet there. They were reduced to such ruses by the feud between her father and Andrew. Julie's remark that any involvement with the putative widow of Stanley Waggoner would enliven the feud gave Gerald pause. But then so did the black-clad woman Bernice showed into his office some ten minutes later.

She floated toward him with her hand extended and Gerald rose to take it. If it hadn't been gloved he might have brought it to his lips. A musky scent enveloped her, a veil hung from her wide-brimmed hat, the black dress seemed to enhance her figure.

"Mr. Andrew Broom?"

"Actually, I am his associate, Gerald Rowan."

She had been in the process of taking the chair he had

directed her to but now she hesitated. But then she did sit and raised her veil with a deliberateness that increased Gerald's desire to see what she really looked like. She was beautiful in a Mediterranean sort of way, olive skin, arched black brows, smooth molded cheeks rounding in the smile that widened her mouth but did not part her lips.

"Associate?"

"Nephew. Partner. Andrew was at the funeral."

"And went on to the cemetery?"

Gerald nodded. "You can either wait until he returns or tell me your business."

"Business." She sighed. "Of course, I am treated like a fraud. I told Stanley that it would be like this, but he promised me he would take care of everything. It seems that he did nothing."

Gerald suggested coffee and after Bernice had served them, he said, "Why don't you just start from the beginning."

"And go on to the end?" She smiled. "Alice in Wonderland."

Gerald let it go. The client is always right.

The beginning had been right here in Wyler, where her grandfather Drexel had been one of the last generation of executives when Waggoner produced automobiles. He had been older than Stanley and it was his task to bring the heir into the management of the company he owned. They remained close even after Drexel went on to the navy and then into the senate.

"The senate?"

"The state senate."

Here in Indiana. Harold Drexel. Subsequently he had become lieutenant governor. His daughter had married the novelist Hershel Morgan. Gerald looked receptive.

"He wrote under the name of Max Gersh."

"Westerns?"

"They were all made into movies. He did very well."

"And you are Max Gersh's daughter."

She smiled. "Yes. My mother left him during the Hollywood years and he developed Alzheimer's. I went to work in the home where he lived. Even so I felt I was abandoning him. But where had he gone?"

Her voice faded away and a sad expression came over her lovely face.

"After he died, I stayed on at Greenview. I had come to know the other old people and I found I did not want to go."

Among them was Stanley Waggoner, and it had been quite by accident that they had discovered their connection through her grandfather. It had brought them close. Stanley was wealthy but he had no one to visit him except those interested in getting some of his money.

"Do you know Frank McGough?" she asked.

"Of course."

"He is a crook."

"I've heard him called that. Why do you think he is?"

"He is a predator. He descended on Stanley and soon learned to come when I was not there to protect Stanley. He persuaded Stanley to change lawyers and become his client."

"On what basis?"

"The Wyler connection. Stanley had been represented by a Chicago firm for years. I suppose they were so large they could absorb the loss of such a client without making too much of a fuss. I urged them to rescue Stanley."

"You spoke to them?"

"A young woman came down. She listened to me but I

could see she saw more trouble than her firm was willing to take on simply to retain a client, however affluent."

"Were you married to Stanley then?"

She looked at Gerald carefully. "Frank McGough will say it is not a true marriage. In a sense he is right, of course. Stanley was an elderly man." She paused on the brink of a delicate subject, then decided that there was no need to spell out for Gerald that she and Stanley had not had a physical love.

"I did love him, though. There are many kinds of love. I transferred to him all the love I had felt for my father, with the difference that Stanley could respond. We spent hours talking."

"But you did marry?"

"Oh, yes. That was Stanley's idea. And it is a legal marriage. It is more than that. We were married by a priest."

"Ah."

"Stanley wanted me to inherit everything. Of course, I told him that was nonsense. What would I do with his money? He actually said that I could rely on Mr. McGough's advice!"

McGough had dismissed her as an impostor from the moment Stanley had died. With his cohorts he descended on the nursing home north of Indianapolis to claim the body and have it flown immediately to Wyler. He had an authorization to do so.

"I followed after, when I learned what had happened." She pressed her shoulders to the back of her chair. "I came to work to find that he was dead and his body already removed."

"Didn't they know you were his wife?"

"No. That was between Stanley and me. I did it for him. I really didn't want to. I think because I could imagine what would be said. It's what I would have thought myself, if it had been another girl. It's a cliché, isn't it? The pushy nurse captivating the senile old millionaire on his deathbed."

"But the marriage was recorded?"

"Father Jim took care of all that."

"Father Jim?"

"Father Jim Campbell. He had given Stanley the last sacraments the day before he died. Thank God for that."

"Stanley was a Catholic?"

"A convert."

Like the marriage, that too had taken place during the last months of Stanley Waggoner's life. And had been kept a secret.

"When I told Mr. McGough that it wasn't right for Stanley to be buried from the Presbyterian church since he had become a Catholic, he warned me not to say a word about it. But he couldn't help smiling."

"Smiling?"

"Obviously he thinks it strengthens his theory that Stanley was taken advantage of in his dotage, that Father Jim and I moved in on him and took him over body and soul."

Gerald had been scribbling away on a yellow pad throughout this and was glad for the distraction. He was committed to Julie, no doubt of that, but he had seldom met a woman to whom he was more immediately attracted.

"What is your age, Mrs. Waggoner?"

"Twenty-seven. And please call me Catherine."

"You want us to represent you and protect your interests as the widow of Stanley Waggoner?"

"Yes."

Gerald was showing her the agreement form when Susannah and Andrew returned from the funeral. Bernice had stepped out, so they did not realize that there was someone with Gerald. They looked from Gerald to the woman and back.

"Mrs. Waggoner, this is Andrew Broom, the senior member of the firm."

8

Rebecca Prell headed for Overlook directly from home when she got the call from the *Dealer* about the girl's body. She had a camera with her and got some shots of the car and of the milling around as they waited for the medical examiner unit from Jasper.

"What was her name?"

"Don't go rummaging around in there, young lady," an old man said, taking Rebecca by the elbow as she was looking into the car.

"I'm Rebecca Prell from the *Dealer*."

"And I am Alex Hollister, town constable."

"You're just the one I'm looking for. What do you know so far?"

The prospect of speaking for the record mollified the old

man and he was happy to tell her what he knew, which was pretty much nothing. Meanwhile, Rebecca got a shot of the girl in the car, managing not to throw up. What a grisly scene.

"My procedure from this point . . ." Alex Hollister was saying, when Rebecca noticed the woman with an overbite and rounded eyes who had gotten out of a golf cart and gone up to the car. Rebecca joined her.

"Who was she?"

The woman turned, her face pale. "Helga. Helga Bjornsen. She worked here last summer."

"Doing what?"

"On the grounds crew. Mowing . . ." She put a hand to her mouth. "I just can't believe this."

"Why did she quit?"

"She went back to school. It was just a summer job."

"She didn't come back this year?"

The woman shook her head. "She had a far better job downtown."

Rebecca got the woman's name, Gladys Winter. She was both reluctant and eager to give it.

"Where did Helga live?"

"I don't know the exact address. With her mother, though."

How many Bjornsens could there be in the Wyler directory? Had her family been told? Had they reported her missing? Rebecca took down the license number of the car. Gladys didn't know if it had been the dead girl's vehicle. The sheriff's deputy on duty didn't know if anyone had been reported missing.

"You mean this girl?"

"For example."

"I don't think so."

"Could you find out?"

"After the funeral."

"After the funeral!"

He grinned. "The Waggoner funeral. It's going on right now."

"Oh, sure."

Stanley Waggoner, reminder of the past grandeur of Wyler, Indiana. Foster, the editor of the *Dealer*, had become almost eloquent when he spoke of what the Waggoner family had done for Wyler.

"Thank God they failed eventually. This would have been nothing but a company town."

Rebecca had learned not to respond sarcastically to such remarks. Foster, like many citizens of Wyler, was convinced that the town was a little bit of paradise where Americans could still live as Americans were meant to live. It was not entirely preposterous. Rebecca had been here two years and still had the feeling she had stepped into a Norman Rockwell painting. That was just the surface, of course. As a reporter she had learned what often lay behind the facade of midwestern peace and prosperity. The murdered girl in the vehicle parked in the cemetery was an instance of the dark side of Wyler.

How many murders had there been since she came here? Several. Well, more than one. And how many arrests, let alone convictions? Wyler was like the rest of the nation in that most crimes went unpunished, particularly violent ones. It was an eerie thought that there were people around who had literally gotten away with murder. And how many slain women went unaccounted for nationwide? When some mad murderer was caught there was an obscene effort to blame a dozen other murders on him, get them off the books. Rebecca suspected that there was something macho in such a murderer's willingness to take on whatever murders the police wished to pin on him. Rebecca Prell made a vow to herself that the death of Helga Bjornsen would not go unavenged.

The Bjornsen address was on the west side of town, an unpaved drive and a front lawn that was largely dirt. A massive willow brooded over the small frame house that had not seen a new coat of paint in years. Rebecca glanced at her watch. It was after nine-thirty but she had the feeling that the house was not yet awake. In fact, it looked permanently asleep, as if years ago it had entered some parenthesis from which it had yet to emerge.

Rebecca parked in the street but did not turn the key so that the ceaseless blather of the radio news could continue. Not that she really expected to learn anything from the radio about the story she was on. The station had decided to follow the funeral of Stanley Waggoner blow by blow. The burial of the dead, coming to you live from WBSW. Rebecca got her phone out of her purse and dialed Foster.

"Her name is Helga Bjornsen, and . . ."

"Who?"

"The girl found dead at the cemetery. And don't say it. The body was in a parked vehicle. I got on it straight from home."

"Helga Bjornsen?"

"Do you know who she is?"

Foster paused but she was patient. He had an annoying habit of falling into periods of silence while he slowly sorted out the inventory of his mind.

"She'd been working for Andrew Broom this summer," he said finally.

"Last summer she worked at Overlook Cemetery."

"I didn't know that."

She told Foster she was parked outside the Bjornsen house on West Brisky. "It doesn't look like anybody's up. Maybe they haven't even missed her yet."

"Find out."

"Sure."

But getting out of the car, she wished she were Foster downtown telling a reporter to knock on that door rather than the reporter who had been told to do it. Not that she wouldn't have anyway. It was just that she wanted Foster to know that she was on the story so that he wouldn't put Piggie on it.

Ross Pigot was Rebecca's bête noire. A summer intern, over six feet tall with dreamy good looks and brains and skill to go with them. He had it in him to become the journalist of his generation. All he lacked was ambition.

"I don't know," he had said when she asked him where he would apply next year when he was a senior and about to go on the job market. She both hoped and feared he would say, "Why, right here at the *Wyler Dealer*. What better place to hone my skills and get ready for the jump into the big time?" What he actually said was, "I'm still trying to make up my mind if this is what I want to do."

"Don't knock it until you've tried it."

But he did not catch the irony. He had spent the last five weeks doing almost nothing. He would have been content to edit obituaries and work on classifieds if Rebecca hadn't insisted that he come along with her on the Carter story. It was the dumbest thing she ever did. She had done all the work and Piggie had been at most a slightly interested companion, but at the end it was to Piggie that Carter had spilled his guts. The nitwit hadn't even taken notes while Carter went into detail on how he had embezzled $150,000 from the local credit union.

"I have a photographic memory," Piggie explained.

"For numbers?"

"For everything. It is my curse."

And he sat down and wrote in a simple readable way the complicated story of a financial shell game, complete with amounts and dates, that was a dazzler. Rebecca could have killed him.

"You are a natural reporter."

He looked sad, as if she had hit upon his hidden flaw. Rebecca certainly didn't want Ross Pigot along on this story. This was hers. Already it was assuming the nature of a crusade, as if she had been picked to vindicate the death of Helga Bjornsen.

The rusty screen in the front door bulged outward and the hook was not in the eye. Rebecca pulled the screen door open, saw that the doorbell was out of commission, and knocked. She put her ear to the panel and listened but there were no sounds from within. She wondered if Foster knew anything more about Helga than that she was working in Andrew Broom's office this summer. She knocked again, more loudly, using the heel of her hand. From somewhere came the conviction that the door would not be opened. She depressed the handle and put pressure on the door and it began to give. She kept pushing until it was open enough for her to slip inside if she decided to do that.

"Hello, hello. Is anyone home?"

She immediately regretted the chuckleheaded cheerfulness

of her tone. If anyone was home, she was bringing them terrible news. She went inside and found herself in a mess. The furniture was okay, it wasn't that, but it might just have been strewn around the room by a careless hand. Surfaces were dusty, the mirror over the fireplace hung slightly askew, the odds and ends on the mantel looked as if they had not been touched in years. Various sections of a newspaper lay on the sofa. Rebecca picked one up to see how old it was.

"What in hell are you doing?"

Rebecca turned to face a woman who held a robe tightly around her. Her gray hair was wild on her head and her eyes glittered with indignation.

"I'm Rebecca Prell of the *Dealer*. Are you related to Helga Bjornsen?"

"What kind of question is that?"

"I have some very serious news about Helga."

Indignation gave way to wariness. "What kind of news?"

"She is dead."

It was possible to think that the woman had not heard. Her expression did not change. She looked at Rebecca as if she were waiting for her to speak rather than absorbing what she had just said. Then she began to sink slowly to the floor. Rebecca caught hold of her and eased her onto the couch, trying to brush away the newspaper first, but the woman sat to the sound of paper crumpling beneath her. A strange humming sound came from her. In a moment it turned into a whimpering cry.

"What happened to her? What happened to Helga?"

Rebecca sat next to her, feeling ghoulish, but this was the moment to get what information she could. The woman nodded when Rebecca asked if she were Helga's mother.

"Adoptive mother," she added.

"How old is she?"

"She just turned twenty-one a week ago. What happened? Tell me what happened."

"She was a student?"

"Yes. In Bloomington."

"When did you last see her?"

The woman rubbed her eyes and sat back. "Yesterday. No, the day before yesterday. I don't always see her before she goes off to work."

"You didn't see her last night?"

"I was out."

A whole history of moral weakness seemed packed into the remark. The woman smelled of last night's drink and before being hit with the news about Helga there had been a pathetic defiance about her. Rebecca could imagine her in a bar, trading stories of injustices she had suffered with other marginal types. There was a subculture of lower-middle-class honky-tonking in Wyler of which Rebecca had only slowly become aware. Foster's official and idyllic picture of the town had obscured such truths for some time.

"Tell me about it. I'm ready now."

"Are you all alone here?"

She seemed to give it some thought. "Yes."

"Is there someone we could call to be with you?"

Her face went blank, as if she were mentally examining the roll call of her friends and finding it empty.

"I'll do that. Tell me about Helga."

Rebecca traded gruesome details of the scene at Overlook Cemetery for facts about the girl's life. Not that there were many. She had been raised in Wyler, attended local schools, had done well both academically and athletically and gone on to the state university, where she was majoring in communications.

"She is a wonderful girl. She deserved more than this." A tragic expression. "And more than me."

"Did she own a car?"

The car that Mrs. Bjornsen described was not the vehicle in which the body of Helga had been found.

Rebecca did not leave until Mrs. Bjornsen had made several phone calls and someone was on the way.

"I was afraid I'd get stuck with her. But she's family."

"Do you have other children?"

"No, thank God. I mean, I'm not cut out for it. I never was."

A second cousin who looked like a hanging judge arrived. Her name was Amity Axelson, and before she came Mrs. Bjornsen told Rebecca that she was known as Battle.

"But don't call her that."

Walking out to her car, Rebecca realized that Mrs. Bjornsen had shown no interest in seeing her daughter. She had not asked where the body was or manifested any sense of responsibility. What kind of girl would come out of a background like that? Her mother's flattering, even awed, account of Helga notwithstanding, Rebecca found herself thinking of Helga as a junior version of the ruined woman in the unpainted frame house with the bulging rusted screen door and a grievance against the world.

She headed downtown, drove into the garage beneath the Hoosier Towers, and took the elevator to the floor where Andrew Broom had his offices. When she pushed through and saw Piggie talking with the receptionist, Rebecca had murderous thoughts of her own.

10

Andrew's first reaction to the putative widow Waggoner
was that she had the look of a woman who might take
advantage of an old man whose mental powers were dwin-
dling. She seemed a composite of those spring blossoms that
regularly appear on the arms of aging swains who just happen to have enormous fortunes. What precisely interested
such decrepit Romeos in these lovely young things was one of
those mysteries of life Andrew hoped to live long enough to
explore. But two minutes with the young woman changed his
mind.

"You are legally married to Stanley Waggoner?"

"Until his death, yes."

"And, if it came to that, you could prove it?"

"I have a license."

"All that being so, you do of course have claims on your husband's estate."

"That's nice, of course, but I deeply resent being treated as if I had just crawled out from under a rock and was telling lies about Stanley and me."

"Who has treated you in that way?"

"Stanley's lawyer."

"Francis X. McGough?"

"Is the X his signature?"

Andrew laughed. "That's good. It may stand for Xerox."

But Susannah broke in, sounding a trifle scandalized. "It stands for Xavier. Francis Xavier. He was a Jesuit."

"Frank?"

"Andrew!"

"My wife is a Catholic," he explained to his new client.

"So am I. Stanley and I were married by a priest. I told your son."

Andrew bristled. Son! Did this woman actually imagine he was old enough to have a son Gerald's age? He looked at Susannah, who was suppressing a smile. Did she regard this as divine retribution for his maligning St. Francis Xavier?

"I suppose McGough drew up the will."

"One of them."

"How many are there?"

"Stanley wrote out another one after our marriage. He said it would consolidate my claim."

"He wrote it out by hand?"

"Yes."

"You saw him do it?"

"No. But he had it witnessed by a doctor and by Father Jim. The priest who married us."

"Where is it?"

She opened her purse and reached in.

"You have it with you?"

She looked at him, surprised. "Don't you want to see it?"

"Of course."

"That's why I brought it."

Andrew had Susannah log it in, make a copy, and put the original in the office safe. "Gerald should put that in the safety-deposit box."

As if on demand, Gerald appeared in the doorway, a stunned expression on his face. He passed a piece of paper to Susannah, who read it and turned to nod at Gerald. Then she said to Andrew, "Gerald just heard about Helga."

Catherine Waggoner looked from one member of the firm to the next. "Who is Helga?"

"It's an entirely different matter," Susannah assured her. "Helga was a summer intern in our office."

Andrew was happy to turn Catherine over to Susannah's gentle care while he read over the handwritten document the widow had taken from her purse. Gerald remained in the office.

"Helga's been murdered!"

Andrew nodded. "I saw the body early this morning. Alex Hollister called me and I went out to Overlook Cemetery, where the body had been found."

"She was killed?"

"Horribly. Her throat had been slashed."

Gerald sank into a chair. "I took her out a few times."

Half of Andrew's motivation in hiring Helga was to provide Gerald with a distraction from Julie McGough. The first unstated reaction on both his part and Susannah's when the dreadful news came that morning was that Gerald had been thrown together with the young woman. Foster of the *Dealer* had recommended her to Andrew when it became clear that he had no room for another summer intern at the paper. Helga herself had never thought of working in a law office, but she had received high marks from Susannah and Bernice and Gerald during her short time there.

"She worked yesterday, didn't she?"

Gerald nodded. It was a strange thought that an attractive young person like Helga could leave this office and a few hours later be in a situation that ended in her violent death.

"Better call her family and see if there is anything we can do."

"There's only a mother." Gerald made a face but said no more before leaving.

Andrew turned his attention to the handwritten document lying on the desk before him. It consisted of a single sheet of the kind of lined tablet paper on which his mother used to write her letters. "Final Will & Testament of Stanley Waggoner" was printed at the top of the page, the lines of the letters somewhat wavering, but the handwriting itself a marvel, a survival from another age when penmanship was an index of a person's character. Stanley Waggoner, being of sound mind and less sound body, hereby declared inoperative any previous will that conflicted with the provisions of the present one. All of his worldly goods were to pass to his wife, Catherine, who would act as chief trustee of the various gifts and donations he had earlier decided upon. He instructed his lawyer and broker and estate manager to turn over to his widow, Catherine, all the assets, monies, stocks, bonds, and other such items, unless she instructed otherwise. The peroration was edifying.

"Finding myself on the threshold of eternity, I beg God's forgiveness for my sins and praise and thank him for the gift of Catherine, who has brightened the twilight of my life and helped me to concentrate on the one thing needful."

The signature was commensurate with the florid handwriting of the text. It was dated and witnessed by Marie Quatern, R.N., and Father James Campbell. It looked pretty good to Andrew. He picked up the phone.

"Susannah, make an appointment for me with Judge Glacer."

"In probate court?"

"I want to file Stanley Waggoner's last will and testament as soon as possible."

A minute later Susannah told him that Judge Glacer would see him immediately.

"I hope I beat Frank McGough to the punch."

11

Hanson from the IBI flew into the Wyler airport before noon and was met by Sheriff Cleary.

"I feel I just left here," Hanson said.

"It's been nearly a year."

Hanson breathed an incredulous sigh. It was his cross to be sent around the state to such places as Wyler where he was regarded as an interfering outsider while at the same time he was expected to answer all questions and solve all mysteries. Wyler bore a disturbing resemblance to the town from which he thought he had escaped long ago to the big city of Indianapolis. It was a relief not to meet a relative around every corner. In Indianapolis he could walk the downtown streets all day and not meet a soul he knew. You had to know his relatives to understand why this seemed such a blessing.

Cleary wanted to tell him about the dead girl and all the rest of it but Hanson stopped him.

"Wait till I see her."

"You might want to have lunch first."

Hanson smiled. That was another thing about the big city. Mayhem and violence were so frequent that he was no longer bowled over by the horrors of his profession.

The crew from Jasper had done a good job. The car had been brought to where it could be subjected to close examination and they had enlisted the coroner to do the autopsy, while discreetly looking over his shoulder to make sure it was all according to Hoyle.

"What about the girl?" Hanson asked Cleary.

"That's her body."

"I know that. What do you know about her?"

"She's a college girl, home for the summer. She was an intern in Andrew Broom's office."

"Andrew Broom!"

"Last summer she worked in the cemetery where the body was found."

"Is it her vehicle?"

"That's quite a story."

The car had been traced to the cemetery employee who had found the body. He now claimed that the vehicle had been stolen, something he didn't realize until he drove up to the car and saw that it was his. He drove a pickup to work and the car should have been in his garage.

"He see it there when he left for work?"

"The garage door was shut. It's a single-stall garage; he leaves the pickup outside."

Cleary said, "You want to talk to Foley?"

"He around?"

He didn't seem to be. Hanson couldn't make head nor tail out of the story of Foley's car, but it sounded fishy as hell. Meanwhile, he was glad for the excuse to call on Andrew Broom. Susannah welcomed him like an old friend, which was nice, but he was there to ask about an employee who had been found murdered that morning.

"Tell me about Helga Bjornsen."

"She was a lovely girl. I still can't believe this has happened."

"Her family live here in Wyler?"

"Her mother."

"Do you know her?"

"I used to," Susannah said. "But I haven't seen her in years. Helga was adopted and I remember when her stepmother decided that ought to be known."

"She announced it?"

"That's a little strong. Of course, people like my folks must have known about it. The thing is, it would be very difficult in a town this size to adopt a child and keep it a secret. Thank God, there is no stigma attached to it anymore."

"Your folks knew her?"

She nodded, but not before hesitating. "They weren't friends or anything. But they knew her, yes."

"You only mention the mother."

"Look, why don't I get out Helga's file?"

"Good."

Susannah had become a little distant during this exchange, as if it had belatedly dawned on her that this was a professional visit. The employment form recorded Helga's educational record and her previous employment. She'd had a paper route in high school, where she had both academic and athletic accomplishments. The previous summer she had indeed worked at the cemetery. Hanson jotted down the Bjornsen address, although he could have found that in the telephone directory. While he was talking with Susannah, Andrew and Gerald came in with a beautiful young woman dressed all in black.

"Mr. Hanson is asking about Helga."

"Oh good," Andrew said, extending his hand to Hanson. "I was hoping they had called you in."

"I understand she was your employee."

"She had been here how long, Susannah, four weeks?"

"Five."

Gerald escorted the lady in black into an office and Andrew drew up a chair. He told Hanson that he personally had no intimation that such a thing could happen to Helga.

"What about boyfriends?"

"Other than Gerald?"

Andrew slid that in easily, and Hanson sensed it was a bit of information he wanted Hanson to get from him.

"They were dating?"

"They went out a few times. Talk to Gerald about it."

"She work out well here?"

Andrew deferred to Susannah on that, and she gave the girl a ringing endorsement. Never late for work, never visibly the worse for wear, as if she had had a big night, perfectly reliable. Gerald joined them.

"But distant. Maybe shy is the word."

"She was beautiful." Gerald said. "Golden hair you wanted to get your hands into. Do you know Yeats's lines to Ann Gregory?"

"You're going to tell me."

" 'Only God could love you for yourself alone, and not

56

your yellow hair.' " Gerald closed his eyes as he murmured the words. He opened them. "There was one great impediment. With her I felt like a middle-aged man. I have a few years before I'm thirty but she thought I was an old man. This was a college girl, all kinds of talent and ambition, but . . ." Gerald touched his head. "There was nothing here. And it wasn't her fault. She had done well in school, but it is a wonder what that can mean nowadays. She did know computers."

"But not Yeats."

"I do sound like a fuddy-duddy, don't I?"

"Where did you take her?"

"To the club. Both times."

"Just twice."

"I'll let you in on a little gossip. Andrew hoped that I would fall for Helga and forget all about Julie McGough."

"It didn't work?"

Gerald made a face. "My idea was to make Julie jealous enough to defy her father's embargo."

"On you?"

"On anything having to do with Andrew Broom."

"Did that work?"

"She wasn't at the club when I took Helga there. And if she heard about my dining with this golden-haired vision she said nothing about it."

"What exactly did the girl do here?"

"Computer stuff. Susannah can explain."

"Who else did she go out with?"

"I never asked."

"Did she go out?"

"Oh, she had to. You'd have to see her."

"I have."

"I meant alive."

"I get the picture, even from her dead."

In a rental car, Hanson drove to the Bjornsen address, where his knock was not answered. He walked around the house and looked at the backyard, which was a mess. The house was in poor repair. The garage door seemed to be off its track and gaped at the side. There was a car inside.

"What do you want?"

"Mrs. Bjornsen?" He showed her his identification. "I'm very sorry about your daughter. I am here to discover what exactly happened and to bring whoever did it to justice."

She reached out and took his billfold and studied the identification. When she handed it back, she said, "I already talked to the police."

"The sheriff?"

"No. Someone from the constable's office."

"When was that?"

"After the reporter was here."

Cleary had not mentioned the constable's involvement. One of the oddities of Wyler was the anachronistic office of constable with its two deputies. Hanson did not like the idea of several inquiries going on simultaneously, but what harm could it do? He was less interested in quizzing the mother than seeing where the girl had lived.

"Did you tell the constable what young men your daughter was seeing?"

"Any boyfriends she had was at college. She never showed a lot of interest in local boys."

"But they must have been attracted to her."

A wistful smile briefly illumined the drawn face. "It takes two to tango."

She moved past him and stooped to take hold of the garage door, but Hanson pulled it up for her, something that required an effort.

"That should be fixed," she said, but it was just an observation. The door was power driven, or meant to be, but it was on the fritz and the rollers were off the runners. Hanson jiggled the rollers into place and the door moved more easily. He got no thanks from Mrs. Bjornsen. She said, "I have to go to the undertaker's."

"Is there anyone to go with you?"

"I can handle it."

In her fashion perhaps, as she had handled her life, and this house, and her daughter. Hanson himself headed for Overlook Cemetery. He wanted to have a talk with Will Foley.

Foster received an imperious call from Frank McGough demanding that he send over a reporter so that the authentic story of the late Stanley Waggoner could be presented to the citizens of Wyler.

"Haven't you been reading recent issues, Frank?"

"Great stuff, great. Right out of the archives. A thorough and accurate picture of the contributions the Waggoner family has made to this community. I am speaking of more recent events."

"The funeral will be written up, Frank. Have no fear."

"The will is about to be contested!"

"By whom?"

"That is what I want to talk about."

Belatedly it occurred to Foster that he represented what for better or worse was one of the most powerful institutions of society, the free press. An equivocal phrase, no doubt: he was not giving away copies of the *Dealer*, nor was it an inexpensive matter to put out the paper, particularly in a time when readers were decreasing and viewers increasing. The future awaiting the newspaper sometimes seemed to promise little more than captions for the pictures seen on television. Foster had managed to diversify and get into television locally and there were those who predicted that one day the paper would close and only the station continue. But whether read or seen, the news and those who supplied it were in the catbird seat. And in this instance, it was clear that Frank McGough needed him far more than he needed Frank McGough.

"I'll be free in an hour, Frank."

"Fine. I can see you then."

"Just give your name at the desk and they'll bring you right up."

Foster savored the silence in which the sizzle of Frank McGough's ego was all but audible. "I'll be there," Frank said gruffly.

Foster dialed Andrew Broom and was told he was with a client. "Susannah, Frank McGough is coming to see me in an hour to talk about Waggoner's will. He sounded as if there were going to be a contest. Andrew know anything about this?"

"Mr. McGough may be referring to the client Andrew is with. Mrs. Stanley Waggoner."

"Mrs. Who?"

"The woman Stanley married some months before his death. But you will want to talk with Andrew. Why don't I have him call you when he's free?"

"I'd like to see him before Frank gets here."

"Come right now and I'll squeeze you in."

Whatever advantage he had gained with McGough had been lost with Broom. He had half a mind to send Rebecca Prell over to get the story. But she was working on the murder of Helga Bjornsen and he didn't want to divert her. Actually, he preferred her working on stories in which he was not involved. She had a way of conveying vague disapproval of the way he ran the paper and while such an attitude from such a fledgling reporter should have carried no weight at all with him, he had been and was infatuated with the saucy young woman. Infatuated as in "fat." He was overeating like a teenager in compensation for his confusion over what he felt for Rebecca. To his dismay, she had proposed a human interest series on the way in which older men become foolishly enthralled with young women.

Of course, he could send Ross Pigot, but even to think the thought was to reject it. The boy had quantities of unused talent but, given his indolence, it was likely to remain unused. Foster sometimes thought he resisted the impulse to fire Pigot and let him relax on his own time only because he knew Rebecca was annoyed with Ross. She exemplified the energetic use of such talent as she had while Ross was stuck on one of the ledges of Mount Purgatory.

Rebecca's theory about younger women and older men recurred when Foster met Catherine Waggoner and heard the story of her marriage to the aged Stanley. Rebecca would not have been a bit surprised.

Rebecca had never thought of a cemetery as a business before. She had stopped in the office and asked who could tell
her about Helga, and Gladys Winter was the soul of cooper-
ation.

"Did you get to know her at all?"

"Me? I sit in here all day and she was usually out on a
mower. I'd see her when she came in the morning and again
at night. We had lunch together a couple of times."

"Where?"

"The McDonald's up the road. I know, I know. Junk food.
She was trying to get her bearings."

"How so?"

"She attracted men."

"So what was the problem?"

Gladys laughed. "All the men who work here are married. Even whozits." She hunched a shoulder toward the sexton's office.

"You're talking about men on the maintenance and grounds crew?"

Gladys nodded her head slowly, as if encouraging Rebecca to get the point. The point seemed to be that a married man, or married men, had come on to Helga while she worked at Overlook. The fact that her slain body had been found there seemed another piece of the puzzle in the game Gladys was mentally playing.

"Why don't we go to McDonald's for lunch? On me."

Meaning on the paper. Gladys was on her feet before Rebecca had finished. She must have weighed about ninety-eight pounds. She was worried about junk food?

It took a Big Mac and large fries to limber up Gladys's tongue to the point where she was willing to talk names.

"All this is guessing, understand. I never actually saw anything."

Rebecca let that go. "Who?"

"The man who found the body."

"Foley?"

A nod. "Will Foley. That was his car the body was found in."

"It was!"

"He reported it stolen." Gladys made a face.

"Do you think there was something between him and Helga?"

"Let's say I think that's what he had in mind."

"And he's married."

"To a friend of mine!"

Whoops. Suddenly the whole line of inquiry seemed tainted by Gladys's motives. Not that Rebecca knew what they were. But all this circling to get to Foley and then the fact that Gladys knew the Mrs., well, it didn't ring true.

"What others?"

"I'm not as sure of the others. I mean, so they look. She was pretty hard not to notice."

Rebecca imagined Gladys with her nose pressed to the window of the sexton's office, looking out at all the men noticing Helga, men who never noticed her, men married to her friend.

"It must be something, the only woman in the bunch. Sort of like a locker room."

Gladys snorted. "Don't worry. I can handle myself."

"Want another?"

"I better not. I feel like I should bathe after this one."

She took Gladys back to the office and asked for the address of Will Foley.

"You going to question him?"

"About the body he found? Sure."

"He's right here now."

"In case I don't find him."

Gladys thought a bit. "Well, it's in the phone book anyway."

"You're just saving me some trouble."

Rebecca was amazed at the different things people did for a living, even here in Wyler. Imagine being stuck in the office of a cemetery sexton ever since high school, surrounded by men who didn't know you were alive. Another funny job was being a deputy to the town constable, like Dwayne Streeter, who was just getting out of his vehicle in front of the Foley address. He adjusted his belt, his trousers, his tie, and squared his hat on his head, then stood, legs akimbo, looking around.

His eye of authority fell on Rebecca as she pulled in behind his car. He rolled slowly toward the driver's door as if the earth was something other than terra firma. He brought two fingers to the brim of his hat.

"Ma'am?"

"Press." She put her hand out the window and pointed at the windshield. Dwayne's eyes narrowed in skepticism.

"I can't let you park here."

"I don't need permission. It's a public street."

"This is a temporarily restricted area."

"You're on duty here?"

"That's right."

"What's happened?"

"You with the *Dealer*?"

Like most cities, large and small, Wyler was a one-paper town. "Yes." She was a little miffed he didn't know who she was. She knew who he was.

"Then you should know of the cemetery slaying."

"But this is Will Foley's house."

"How'd you know that?"

"They told me so where he works."

"The cemetery?"

"Yes."

"Was he there?"

"I didn't see him," she said, and breezed past him to the house. Obviously the sheriff had begun to put two and two together. Will Foley's allegedly stolen car and the body of a girl he had been chasing last summer . . .

* * *

Fiona Foley wore an ankle-length dress and was barefoot. Rebecca was reminded of an early Picasso, wives on the beach, looking out to sea, wondering if their fishermen husbands would return.

"I went to the cemetery but he isn't there, Mrs. Foley."

She waited to see what the significance of this was supposed to be.

"What do you know about the car that was stolen from your garage the night the girl was killed?"

"Talk to Will about that. I don't know one car from another."

"Did you hear anything?"

"Hear what?"

"Someone taking the car from the garage."

"Is that what happened?"

"What do you think happened?"

"You'll have to ask Will."

There were children, clean, well-behaved, clinging to her skirt. She stepped into sandals as she crossed the room to pick up the baby. Rebecca felt like an intruder, disrupting the routine of this household. Was Mrs. Foley really so indifferent to what her husband had been up to?

"I talked to Gladys," Rebecca said. "At Overlook."

"Gladys."

"She said she knew you in school."

"Oh, yes."

But it was unclear if Fiona Foley remembered Gladys or was interested in anything outside her somewhat disordered domestic routine. Rebecca hoped for her sake that her husband wasn't in trouble, but that seemed a thin possibility. Married man playing around with a college girl who had been employed in Overlook last summer. Had he tried to renew the affair and been rebuffed? Had he been with Helga in that car parked in a remote section of Overlook? Apparently the first thing he said when he came to work that morning was that there was a car parked out in the Resurrection section. Reporting his car stolen had been a clumsy attempt to divert attention from him.

Rebecca was filled with sadness thinking of Foley's wife and kids. Too bad he hadn't thought of them more.

In mid-afternoon Andrew took stock with Susannah and Gerald. It had been one helluva day so far and it was not over. It had begun with the discovery of the body of their summer intern in a vehicle parked in Overlook Cemetery and had gone on to the acquisition of a client who looked to have a solid claim on the Waggoner fortune, a fact that provided Andrew with a powerful weapon in his ongoing war with Frank McGough. Glacer had accepted and recorded the will, after ascertaining the identity of Catherine Waggoner and listening to her claim as to her relation to Stanley. Among the items she had in her large purse was the wedding certificate attesting to their marriage.

"I think we can proceed in the usual fashion, Andrew. Were you at the funeral?"

"They humiliated me at the wake," Catherine said, assuming the question was meant for her. "I boycotted the funeral. I will have a Catholic memorial service for my husband."

Glacer clearly did not want to get involved in any quarrels between brands of Christianity.

Gerald went immediately to another judge to get a cease-and-desist order against Francis X. McGough, preventing him from acting in the name of the deceased until the probation of the will Catherine Waggoner had submitted. News of these two legal actions got to McGough, of course, and brought an irate phone call.

"You talk to him, Gerald."

"He demands to talk to you."

"I wouldn't demean myself. You may tell him that. You may also tell him . . ." But then he picked up the phone, to hear the profane and angry voice of Frank McGough. The anger of the man calmed Andrew.

"There are laws about talking on the telephone in that way."

"Andrew!"

"Not that I imagine you have any extensive acquaintance with the law."

"Is it true that you are representing this phony widow?"

"No."

"It isn't true?"

"No. I am, however, representing the genuine widow of Stanley Waggoner, if that is your question. I may very well advise her to take an action against you for your public humiliation of her. As for any further attempts to thwart the will of Stanley Waggoner—"

"Stanley Waggoner is my client! What the hell are you, an ambulance chaser?"

"Well, your client married my client and in a will that has been registered in probate left everything to her."

"The man was nearly senile."

"That he chose you to represent him gives some credence to that, perhaps, but there is no doubt as to his state of mind when he abrogated all earlier wills and left his entire fortune to his widow, Catherine."

The storm was succeeded by an Arctic calm. "You will never pull this off, Andrew. I don't know what ruses you employed to persuade an old man to enter into some sort of bogus ceremony with that predatory nurse, but I will find out. Not only will you lose, Andrew, I will get you disbarred and driven from this town."

The connection was broken. Andrew looked at his wife and nephew.

"The battle is joined."

"Thank you for remaining calm, Andrew."

"Gerald, I want you to hunt up every relevant or near-relevant precedent for such a will."

Gerald was on his feet. "I'll have Helga . . ." He stopped and stared at the others. This was just the sort of task at which Helga had become so good. She was a wizard of the legal database.

"God rest her soul," Susannah murmured.

It was two days later that Andrew said to Gerald, "Call Cleary and see if they know who killed her yet."

Of course, he meant Hanson. Gerald had told him Hanson had been on the go since arriving. Helga's death would be routine for him. He might be on a plane back to Indianapolis tonight. Apparently he had already flown to Bloomington and other points around the state.

"There are several possibilities," Hanson said when Cleary put him on and Andrew asked him if he knew yet who had killed Helga Bjornsen.

"Want to have dinner tonight?" Andrew looked inquiringly at Susannah and she nodded.

"Sounds good."

"At my place. That will give us a chance to talk."

"Will your nephew be there?"

"I can ask him."

"Don't."

That was a disturbing request but nothing in Hanson's manner when he came by the house later betrayed any deep significance in it. They had drinks on the back patio, where Andrew could keep an eye on the grill. Susannah had laid a table in the screened portion of the patio, certain that bugs and mosquitoes would ruin the evening otherwise. Hanson, dressed casually, held his drink in both hands, smiled at husband and wife, busy about their respective chores yet attentive to their guest, and said, "You two could give domestic life a good name."

"Surely you don't need any persuasion?" Susannah said sweetly.

"Let's just say that it gladdens the heart to see you two together."

Andrew happened to know something of the roller coaster Hanson's personal life had taken him on. His second wife had run off a year before with a man with whom she claimed to be meditating transcendentally. The effort to cloak infidelity in a mantle of metaphysics and pseudo-religion had soured the inspector and he was now dubious of any general theory of life.

"Why do we insist on living our lives in front of a mirror?" Hanson asked.

Andrew turned from the grill. "To see who's behind us?"

Hanson roared with delight. Like most skeptics, he was constantly flirting with disguised dogmatism. But his delight in the apparent and real domestic bliss he saw at Andrew's was genuine.

Additionally, the contrast between such normalcy and the world in which his professional life involved him prompted Hanson to seize such moments of tranquility as presented themselves. So very little was as it seemed to be.

"The girl was an enigma," he said some hours later when he and Andrew were seated side by side, Susannah having excused herself so they could have the exchange that Andrew wanted.

"How so?"

"How would you describe her?"

"I already did."

"Right. A college girl home for the summer. A year to go until her degree. Major, communications, whatever the hell that is. She was raised by her mother, her adoptive mother, and seems to have overcompensated for her drab background by excelling in school, in class, on the soccer field. She could have had an athletic scholarship to IU but went there on a Merit. While not on the first team, she played in more than half the varsity soccer games during her freshman and sophomore years. When she returned as a junior, she quit the team."

"I didn't know that."

"Friends found her more pensive last year than previously.

One of them spoke of it as resigned, as if she had just found out how things really are and had come to terms with it."

"She spent the summer before her junior year working in the cemetery."

"She wrote poetry."

"You've found out quite a bit."

" 'The World Is a Cemetery' is the title of one."

"A bit lugubrious. Have you seen it?"

"Her mother has been very cooperative."

"Did she have a love life?"

"That phrase dates you, Andrew, but the answer is equivocal. Despite her changed attitude, her social life in Bloomington seems to have accelerated during her junior year. Nothing bacchanalian and no special boy, but out a lot, sought after as lots of fun, able to live it up and still do well as a student."

"But no more soccer."

"It's one of the reasons she gave for quitting sports. She had given half a dozen years to a Spartan life and wanted a few normal student years before she had to enter the real world."

"The real world," Andrew said, directing a pensive row of smoke rings from his cigar into the night. Darkness had fallen and out on the lawn, like miniature planets in a diminished universe, fireflies flickered sporadically in the night. "That came down to interning in my office."

"There was more to her life than that."

"Oh."

"The reason I didn't want Gerald here, I don't know how serious he was about the girl. She led something of a double life."

"Gerald took her out a couple of times. I had hoped something might develop, but it hadn't."

"I think I will take one of those cigars now."

Hanson had refused the offer when they settled down with the postprandial drinks to get at the point of the evening meeting. When he had the cigar prepared and lighted and Andrew had freshened their drinks, he sighed.

"Last year in Bloomington Helga became involved in something that very nearly ended her academic career. She signed up for a course in photography advertised in the student paper, but not a course connected with the university."

The faint aroma from the grill still rode the night air. The pulsing light of the fireflies continued, a metaphor of the brevity of life.

"It was the device of a producer of skin flicks to enlist college girls in his films."

The so-called photography course had represented a staged seduction of the hitherto innocent, the breaking down of their natural resistance by a gradual descent from the daring to the equivocal to the increasingly overt. Hard-core was right around the corner.

"Helga took part as an actress?" Andrew's image of the well-scrubbed wholesome young intern was shaken by what Hanson was saying.

"That's where it's equivocal. It was Helga who went to the prosecutor. Apparently she finally saw what was going on, assumed it was illegal as well as immoral, and decided to put a stop to it."

"And?"

"The prosecutor soon found he was dealing with real pros.

Everything involved was consensual, and raunchy as the eventual products were, there is no longer a law against it. Did you know we fought the war to make the world safe for pornography, Andrew?"

"So nothing happened?"

"Not to the porno producer. But films featuring Helga were soon available gratis to fraternity houses. Her claim was that innocent scenarios in which she had figured—in the nude, however—had been ingeniously spliced into hard-core action so that it looked as if she herself had engaged in orgies."

"Did she sue?"

"The prosecutor advised against it. I don't know if she spoke with any other lawyers."

"I wish to God she had spoken to me."

"Maybe that's what she intended to do, eventually."

Andrew was assailed by the thought that he had not made any such revelation easy. He had treated Helga as what she appeared to be and, he firmly believed, basically was, and that would not have been conducive to her unburdening herself about her brush with pornography.

"Are you suggesting that Helga's death is tied up with this?"

"I'd be a damned fool not to think so, wouldn't I?"

"Yes."

Fiona just looked at Will when she found out who the girl was he had found dead at work. It was a fight she thought she had won, he supposed, but the truth was Helga had left him, not the reverse. Even saying she'd left him made it sound like more than it was. What had there been, after all? One or two times, and that was it. He had never understood her anyway. She was looking for something that just wasn't there.

"Whenever I think of your wife I could cry," she had said.

"I know what you mean."

She drew back, shocked. And he learned a lesson. She saw them as involved in some tragic and doomed affair. She was willing to give him everything and he was in no position to accept. He had a wife, he had children, she was the invader of domestic peace, the evil principle, the temptress. She wouldn't have believed him if he told her that Fiona's policy was to know as little as possible and hope all problems were temporary. She had never really expected that he wouldn't cat around a bit. Men were like that. But by and large, they came back and settled down and the less said the better. She made it almost too easy.

But Helga made it too difficult. What a summer they could have had if only she had been willing to take advantage of opportunities as they presented themselves. My God, that was the excitement of it. Spontaneous, out behind the mausoleum with the air rich with the smell of clover and the planes going over on the landing pattern to the airport, the whole thing natural. But Helga wanted every time to be a major event, the culmination of hours of what she refused to call foreplay— "It is courtship, not play!" Of course, he acted as she wanted. Whatever it took was all right with him, just so long as it ended up right, but they had missed chance after chance because of her demand for the dramatic. He was almost glad to see her go off at the end of summer. He had assumed that their farewell would be one final go at it. He could still see her sad little smile as she shook her head.

"I have led you astray enough."

"I'll be the judge of that."

"Go back to your wife, Will. Forget this awful summer . . ."

"Awful?"

"Yes. This has been a vacation from your true self, Will. We have both been on vacation. And now it is over."

No wonder he had started seeing Regina even before Helga went back to Bloomington.

Regina was more like what he wanted in a woman. Unlike

Helga, she seemed to have no reluctance at all to take it when they could. He had more of her in a week than he had of Helga during a whole summer. She was the sister-in-law of one of Fiona's best friends. Fiona didn't have friends, she had best friends. Regina's husband was a foot doctor who worked out of his house, and that made getting away pretty attractive to her. They met on bingo night at the VFW. That's what she called him. Bingo. The first thing she had said when they were introduced was Bingo. There was nothing bashful about her where he was concerned.

Sometimes during the day, riding the big mower over an undeveloped section, just cutting back the weeds, letting the thoughts jostle around in his head with the movement of the machine, it seemed to Will that a man owed it to himself to get as much as he could. Within the circumstances of his own life. God knows what he would do if he won the lottery and had millions. He would probably burn himself out in a couple of months, rent the Playboy mansion and just work his way from room to room. Since that was unlikely, he had to pursue the ideal in an attainable way. That meant not rocking the boat too much, keeping his eyes open and making a move when opportunity presented itself. As it had on bingo night at the VFW.

They sat bun to bun on a bench, giving only half a mind to their cards. He had her the first time that night, in the parking lot, in the backseat of the car.

"We're like a bunch of kids," she said, but she loved it.

"If I were a kid I'd ride a motorcycle."

"How do they do it?"

"They get off."

"But how?"

What a rascal she was. The next week they drove to the dunes and did it in the sand with only a blanket over them, people not all that far away, but what the hell. It was like a honeymoon. "Beach blanket bingo," she said. "The movie. I never read the book."

"Was there a book?"

"Do you realize you have hammertoes?"

"So what?"

"You didn't know, did you?"

"You're married to the foot doctor, not me."

She sighed.

There was a special school in Chicago where he had learned the trade. "He's a real doctor?"

"A foot doctor. And he married a Bunyan. That's his joke."

Well, why not, it was an age of specialization. Dentists worked on teeth, brain surgeons on brains, cardiologists on hearts, eye doctors on eyes.

"And tree doctors on trees."

Regina made forgetting about Helga fairly easy, although there were times when he missed the teasing reluctance of the younger woman. And her golden hair. It had changed subtly throughout the summer under the influence of the sun and being outside all day, but as it became more bleached her skin tanned and she took on a new and in some ways more attractive beauty. If she had not gone back to school Will sometimes felt he would have learned more of the subtleties of the relation between man and woman.

It was to Regina that he fled on the day he found Helga's body in the car parked in the Resurrection section. In his own car. When Gladys came up in the golf cart and he looked again at the car in which Helga lay dead he noticed the license number. Jesus! The pickup he had driven from the maintenance shed was parked behind the constable's car. How had he failed to see the car was his own? It was a common make, a Honda Civic. Cars of the same make were identical, if you didn't look too close, but somehow you always knew your own. He felt like a dummy when he noticed the plate.

"She worked there?" Regina was trying to understand what he was saying. She was about to take her kids to day care and it was hard to talk so he went with her, bouncing along in the four-wheel-drive while the kids ricocheted around in back, yelling and screaming, having the time of their lives. Regina watched them flee up the walk to the entrance of day care with a wistful expression.

"Can you imagine our mothers unloading us like this every day, Will?"

"My mother didn't work."

"I work graveyard. I could swing it. I could give them my day."

Sometimes he picked her up at midnight when she finished at Webb Tool & Die and they had a few drinks, driving separately to the bar and parting in the lot afterward. They talked some more of his finding Helga's body.

"I used to date her, you know."

"Is that right?"

"This was way last summer. She went back to school. I hadn't seen her for a year."

Almost true, but not quite. He had parked outside her mother's house a couple of times in June, hoping to run into her, and once he telephoned but he couldn't understand Mrs. Bjornsen. And then, downtown, he saw her go into the Hoosier Towers and double-parked but by the time he got inside she was gone. The elevators were run by attendants, one a handicapped woman who sat on a stool in her car.

"Did a girl with yellow hair just go up?"

The attendant nodded.

"Do you know what floor she got off on?"

"All the way to the top."

The building directory had only one listing for the twelfth floor. Andrew Broom.

He beat it outside in time to persuade a meter maid not to give him a ticket. "It was an emergency."

"Yeah?" Her red hair seemed unnatural and she wore her uniform like a Halloween costume. She chewed gum as if she were thinking.

"I saw this girl and I wanted to say hello."

"That's urgent?"

"It is with me."

She shifted her gum and straightened the name plate that was tilted up at him by her breast. L. Z. Bell.

"What's the L. Z. stand for?"

"They call me Lazy."

"Shame on them."

She tore off the ticket and handed it to him. She had scrawled a phone number on the back. He never did call her. Now, that gum-chewing meter maid seemed a threat. He could imagine her recounting the scene: "He left his car in the middle of Tarkington and ran into a building after the girl." The handicapped operator would get off her stool and point a gnarled finger at him. "That's the one! That's him." Looking at the lifeless body of Helga he'd had the craziest thought that he was responsible for her death.

"What if they start asking, Gina? You know? Why in the

82

cemetery? And they'll learn she worked there, they already know that, and then someone is going to remember that she and I . . ."

"Who you worried about, the police or your wife?"

"I'm not worried!"

She opened her arms and there was nothing between them but his T-shirt and hers when he hugged her to him. Her warm breasts convinced him he really wasn't worried. Just because a girl he had been catting around with last summer had been found in his car in the cemetery where he worked and he had discovered the body and didn't say right away it was his vehicle, he should worry?

"You're shivering," Gina said.

16

Hanson was glad he had conveyed to Andrew Broom that his nephew Gerald was as much under suspicion as Will Foley, though he doubted that the lawyer believed him. Gerald said he had taken Helga Bjornsen to the country club on the few occasions they had gone out, and the bartender remembered her well.

"I knew right away she was not the country club type." The bartender's nose wrinkled when he spoke and when he had finished it twitched before settling into repose.

"What do you mean?"

"Natural. She noticed me. For most of the members, I'm invisible. Same with their guests. But she noticed me."

"Sounds like you noticed her too."

"Beautiful hair. Golden. Who's the girl in the story, Rumpleskin, something like that?"

Will Foley, on the other hand, had a reputation as a ladies' man. Not only that, he had discovered the body lying dead in his own car, which he then decided had been stolen. He was either stupid or wise as a fox.

Hanson drove out to the cemetery, parked in a visitor's spot and went into the office, where the air-conditioning was frigid. They could store bodies in there. The girl with the overbite looked up at him and a moment passed before she recognized him.

"Oh. Inspector . . ."

"Hanson. Did everyone come to work today?"

"Whom do you have in mind?"

"Will Foley."

"He's out there somewhere." She made an expansive gesture.

"Did he say anything to you about his car being stolen?"

"He reported it on that phone. As soon as he came in from finding the body."

"That was his vehicle the girl was found in."

Gladys just looked at him. No comment.

"Was there anything between him and the girl? I mean last summer, when she worked here."

"How would I know?" But her expression conveyed another message. He sensed an eagerness in her so he continued putting questions.

"I suppose there's nothing to it."

"To what?"

"Sometimes people say things and—"

"It's true! As long as you've heard it from others I'll tell you. He had it bad for her, followed her around like Mary's little lamb, and they saw one another."

"He's married, right?"

"Right or wrong, he's married."

"All this was last summer?"

"As far as I know."

"Well, she went back to school and he went on working here."

"And his attention was diverted."

"Ah."

"I won't say anything because I'm not sure."

"It might be the biggest favor you could do him."

"Favor?"

"Things that look bad often turn out to mean nothing. I mean, I don't approve of a married man fooling around, but it isn't a capital offense. Maybe the new girlfriend would be just the alibi he needs."

"Regina Foote." She said it like a ventriloquist, trying not to use her lips, as if then she really wasn't saying it.

"I suppose she's in the book."

"I'll look it up for you."

She did and then turned the book toward him, giving him a slip of paper. "Did Will drive to work this morning?"

"That's his Chevy pickup." She pointed. "The red one."

"Tell me about Regina Foote."

She shook her head. "She's a friend of mine. I'm already sorry I said what I did."

"That she and Will Foley . . ."

"You said she might give him an alibi."

She made it sound as if her friend would lie for Will Foley. "Does she know he's married?"

"So is she."

"Did he ever make a pass at you?"

"Will Foley? I should say not."

It was all she could do to keep a severe expression. Someone coughed in the next room and Hanson was surprised.

"Who's in there?"

"Mr. Schmucker. The sexton."

"I'd like to see him."

She marched to the closed door and rapped on it before turning the knob. She stepped inside and almost immediately stepped out again.

"He's not there."

Hanson went to the door and looked in. The inner office was ill lit, blinds pulled, only the computer monitor aglow. A door at the far end of the office led into a maintenance shed.

"Gone," Gladys Winter said.

17

Andrew flew his Cessna to Indianapolis, having made an appointment with the Rev. James Campbell, the priest who had visited the rest home in which Stanley Waggoner had spent his last days. Father Campbell had presided at Stanley's entrance into the Catholic church; he had performed the marriage ceremony that catapulted Catherine from penury to unimaginable wealth; he had witnessed the document in which Stanley had stated his wish that all his worldly goods pass into the hands of his bride. It had occurred to Andrew to take Susannah along. After all, she was the cradle Catholic and could provide sure guidance through whatever lay before him. But in the end he had decided to go alone. One thing seemed as clear as the sky through which he flew: Father Campbell had profited not a whit from executing his priestly duties in these various matters.

"I want to do something for him, of course," Catherine had said when he broached this delicate topic.

"Did you tell him that?"

"Not yet. I suppose I should have, but it would have looked as if . . ."

Andrew nodded. Indeed it might have. "He wouldn't be human if he didn't think that eventually you would decide to make him a gift."

Catherine laughed, a clear bell-like laugh as if she were providing the correct pitch to silver chimes. "He would never take anything for himself. I meant for the parish."

Andrew had to see for himself if this clergyman was as unworldly as Catherine suggested. From the time he had taken her as a client, he had been second-guessing his own every move with the imagined countermove of Frank McGough. Much as he despised the man, he had no delusions about McGough. He was a man of cunning and brilliance, never to be underestimated. In the present contest, the prize was so great that McGough would stop at nothing to insure victory. For him to lose would be to lose control of the immense fortune Stanley Waggoner had almost inadvertently amassed.

"Exactly how much do you think Stanley left you, Catherine?"

"Lots. That's all I know. Stanley himself wasn't sure how much there is. There are trusts and things he wants me to look after, money he has already designated for this and that. But he said there should be quite a bit left for me."

On the basis of a photocopy of the handwritten will and

the knowledge that Stanley Waggoner's widow was Andrew's client, Al Van Blitzen provided Andrew with the rough dimensions of the portfolio he managed for Stanley. The book value of the common and preferred stock was between twenty-nine and thirty million; bonds accounted for another ten million. Al said that Stanley had a futures account with Manley Thomas.

"These monies were largely for fooling around with. Originally, he invested fifteen million with me and told me to use my imagination and daring. He called this money he was willing to lose."

Andrew Broom had been born poor and had become rich by dint of his own efforts—and, of course, some luck—but along the way his conception of money had changed. After a certain point, money became an abstraction, a number on a printout or given over the phone in answer to a question. It fluctuated because of millions of decisions made in thousands of different places. The number could increase appreciably and this caused a sense of satisfaction, but what did the larger number mean? At the outset money purchased things that one needed or wanted, then things that one neither needed nor really wanted, so it was best left to the vagaries of growth. The image of the greedy man is of the miser running gold coins through his fingers, feeling the heft of what is his. But wealth is no longer tangible. It has neither weight nor texture nor taste. The numbers on the printout refer to numbers on certificates that are correlated with other numbers on other printouts.

The difference between the poor man and the rich man remains, but above the poverty line there is little to choose between the comfortable middle class and the multimillionaire. Preparing to meet the otherworldly Father James Campbell, Andrew felt that he himself had become something of an Anchorite about money.

He was cleared for landing and for the next ten minutes was totally absorbed in bringing the aircraft precisely into pattern and descending methodically to the runway. There was the familiar little throb of satisfaction when he felt his wheels once more in contact with the greater curve of the earth. Twenty minutes later, he was in the rental car that was waiting for him and heading west to Terre Coupe.

What had happened to the elm trees of the nation seemed to have bypassed Terre Coupe in some kind of dendrological passover. The main street—named, appropriately, Main Street—was a leafy bower, great elms flanking it at intervals of fifty feet, their branches all but meeting over the thoroughfare. Side streets too were avenues of elms, and on Elm Avenue Andrew found the Church of St. Rose of Lima. It was tannish stucco, a low structure whose tile roof rose gently toward a bell tower topped by a cross. An arcade led from the side of the church to a rectory, also of stucco. The parish school was on the opposite side of the rectory and another arcade connected the two buildings. The lawns were well kept; everything seemed in excellent repair. There was a man in a lawn chair with a book on his lap and a straw hat pulled over his eyes. Andrew passed him as quietly as he could on the way to the door.

"Can I help you?"

"I'm going to the rectory. Do you know if Father James is in?"

"No. He's out. He is in the yard, seated in a chair, supposedly reading his breviary." The man rose and extended his hand. "Welcome to St. Rose."

"You're Father Campbell?"

A little nod. "There is a chair similar to this one on the porch. Or we could sit up there."

Andrew brought the chair and placed it beside the priest. Somehow he had gotten the impression from Catherine that Father Jim was young, but this man was at least sixty. When he took off his hat and put it on his knee, he revealed a high domed head, devoid of hair but adequately fringed on the sides. His were laughing eyes and Andrew immediately felt at ease.

"Catherine Waggoner has engaged me as her lawyer."

He told Father Campbell who he was, and they spent a few minutes locating Wyler on the priest's mental map of the state.

"You knew Stanley Waggoner, Father?"

"I went to see him, yes. Catherine suggested it. He wanted to hear about her Catholicism and seemed to be fascinated. Catherine had the impression that he found it as strange as she would find, well, Mormonism. She had underestimated her own eloquence. He said he would like to talk to a priest about it, so I went over. Of course, I was hesitant to receive him into the church."

"Why?"

"Deathbed conversions almost never happen. When one is old or ill the mind prefers the grooves it has traveled all along. Of course, people can find religion fascinating, in a remote way. But Stanley was different. He wouldn't be put off."

"So he became a Catholic?"

"He did. But he had another surprise in store for me. And

I think for Catherine. He wanted her to be his wife. I drew the line at that."

"They didn't marry?"

"Oh, I had to give in eventually. It wasn't the usual thing."

"What is the usual thing?"

The priest squinted at him and then pulled a pipe from the pocket of the jacket he wore. "If tobacco bothers you, you can get downwind."

In answer Andrew brought out a cigar, prepared and lit it. Again he asked the priest what the usual thing is.

"You're too young to realize it, of course. People grow old, even aged, but one thing never changes. Half of them are men and half of them are women. Gender is destiny. Its biological role has been played out by then, of course, but there are those, usually men, who cannot accept that. They do not want to be eunuchs. Interest in young women, the desire to marry them, is usually just a protest against their debilitated condition. He could have had Catherine's friendship without any ceremony."

"He didn't agree with you?"

"No. Nor in the end did she. Of course, I'm a celibate and observe these matters from a puzzled distance. The attraction of the sexes is a mystery at any time of life. But in the case of Stanley and Catherine . . ." He waved the burning match he held, extinguishing it before it got to his thumb and finger. "Yes, I married them. I decided it could do no harm, and they were both certain that is what they wanted."

"Catherine is a parishioner of yours?"

"She grew up here. Attended the school, then went on to Indianapolis after her parents . . ."

Catherine's family, her parents and two brothers, had been

killed in a dreadful automobile accident on a Memorial Day weekend.

"You will think that has something to do with her marrying Stanley."

"Do you?"

He shrugged. "Perhaps. Who knows?"

"Catherine showed me the will Stanley made out."

The priest tipped back his head and laughed. "I went along with it, of course. Imagine, that old fellow writing out that solemn statement as if he had a fortune to bequeath."

"But he did, Father. He was a very wealthy man."

"Stanley?" He sat forward, searching Andrew's face as if he were sure his visitor was twitting him.

"You didn't know that?"

"My dear fellow, I have several times been asked to witness such documents and they have always amounted to imaginary holdings. Sometimes an old person is simply deluded about his assets and quite sincerely wishes to pass them on. Stanley was such a simple man . . ."

Andrew explained to Father Campbell that there would be strenuous legal efforts to prevent Catherine from coming into her inheritance. "There are others who feel they have a claim."

"Relatives?"

"Distant relatives."

Father Campbell looked serious. "If I had had any idea that others would be badly used because of that piece of paper . . ."

Andrew hastened to explain that it was not that Stanley had left any legitimate claimant unprovided for. On the contrary. It was only the desire of some to have it all that would be thwarted. On that basis Father Campbell was willing to agree that he would testify to the exact circumstances in which Catherine and Stanley married and the will had been drawn up.

"I don't think Catherine had any more idea than I did that there was a real fortune involved."

"The important thing is that Stanley knew. And he made his will known. You found him compos mentis, didn't you?"

"Oh, my yes. He was a delight to talk with. He had been everywhere." The priest shook his head. "I suppose I should have guessed that a man who had traveled so extensively must have had the means to do so." He looked at Andrew. "Have you been to the nursing home? It is a very modest place. Not where you would expect to meet wealthy old folks."

"I will stop there on my way back to Indianapolis."

"Tell them I'll be by the day after tomorrow."

Mrs. Quatern seemed to swim toward him on water wings. She wore white shoes with rubber soles, a white uniform and a white coat sweater that could never have been closed over her ample bosom. During the war pilots had called lifesavers Mae Wests. They might just as aptly be called Mrs. Quaterns.

"I am Andrew Broom. I phoned. About Stanley Waggoner."

"Come in, come in."

She set off down the hallway, her shoes emitting little sucking sounds as she went. She entered an office, rounded the desk, sat and waved him to a chair. "I have fifteen minutes."

"That should be more than enough. You were one of the witnesses of Stanley Waggoner's will."

"His will?"

Andrew described the handwritten document and she

frowned it into remembrance and then laughed. "Oh, sure. Father Campbell and I both went along with it, signing solemnly. He said he would leave something for the home."

"He did."

She tucked in her chin and rested her crossed arms on her bosom.

"One hundred thousand dollars."

"In Monopoly money?"

"How much did it cost Stanley to live here?" She told him. "And you were always paid?"

"Yes. Of course."

"So you must have known he had some money."

It took almost the whole of the fifteen minutes to bring Mrs. Quatern to the realization that she had witnessed a will that transferred unimaginable millions to the nurse who had been on her staff. She fell back in her chair.

"My God in heaven."

"Needless to say, there are those who want to contest the will. You will be asked to describe the exact circumstances in which the will was signed and witnessed."

"But I thought it was a little game."

"Would you have refused to sign if you had known it was not?"

"I never dreamed . . ."

Mrs. Quatern eventually said that, of course, she would testify to these events.

"How much did you say he gave the home?"

"A hundred thousand dollars."

"People will think I signed for the sake of that money."

"People will wonder that you settled for so little."

The golf course at the country club provided one of the tried-and-true trysting places for Gerald Rowan and Julie McGough. Gerald had been present when Andrew and Susannah dined with their new client and Julie had perhaps pardonably thought that Gerald was paired off with Catherine. Understandably this misconception had enhanced Gerald's attractiveness. For a week she had been resisting his suggestion that they meet; now she waylaid him outside the dining room when Andrew was showing Catherine the ancient photographs of the founders.

"I have a one-fifteen tee time tomorrow afternoon," Julie said through her smile.

"You know my Uncle Andrew and Aunt Susannah." Andrew did not like to be referred to in this avuncular fashion. Andrew's pique at Gerald softened the fact that this was the daughter of Frank McGough that he was facing. Susannah, of course, was the soul of cordiality. "And this is Catherine Waggoner."

Catherine smiled sweetly and Julie smiled sweetly back. When she turned toward the dining room, she whispered again, "One-fifteen."

Catherine was staying in the guest suite at Andrew's house. Gerald said good-bye to them in the parking lot, got into his car, waited until they were on their way, and then went back into the club. Waiting until one-fifteen the following day to see Julie seemed more than mortal man was meant to bear. He glanced into the dining room as he went past it on his way to the bar and saw that Julie was still seated with her companions. Who were they? He had been unaware of Julie's presence while he and the Brooms dined with Catherine Waggoner and Julie had come out alone to speak to him. He would take up his post in the bar and catch her when she emerged.

"Terrible about that girl you brought here a few times, Mr. Rowan," the bartender said.

"I still can't believe it."

"They've been here asking about her."

Gerald turned to face the bartender. "What do you mean?"

"An inspector from Indianapolis. He asked if you had brought her here."

"And you remembered?"

He tipped his head to one side. "That golden hair."

Helga had never been in a private club before. Neither, for that matter, had Catherine Waggoner. Unlike Helga, she had been impressed by the club and was surprised when Andrew told Catherine that her grandfather had been one of the founders.

"Stanley spoke harshly of private clubs."

"You discussed them with him?"

"Oh no. He talked. He was always surprising me with the knowledge he had of things. He spoke of exclusive clubs, yacht clubs, alumni clubs, as if he had done a special study of them."

"Doubtless from within," Andrew said.

Catherine still seemed half incredulous that Stanley Waggoner was all she had learned him to be since his death.

"I wonder if he was a member here."

"Willy-nilly."

"What do you mean?"

"Direct descendants of the original founders are de jure and ex officio members of the club. They have no choice in the matter. But I don't think I ever saw him here. I don't believe he played golf."

"Just tennis."

"He told you that?"

"Oh, we played together." She smiled and sipped her wine, leaving them to imagine this lovely young woman matched on the tennis courts against an octogenarian. "He was teaching me the game."

"What'll it be?" Charlie asked now, one eye on Gerald, the other on the television over the bar where a middleweight bout was on. Charlie had boxed in the Golden Gloves when he was a kid and had a proprietary attitude toward the sport.

Gerald asked for beer. If Charlie's attention was now divided, so was his; he kept one eye on the dining room lest Julie leave without his seeing her. A technical knockout and a beer and a half later, she appeared, but she was not alone. In fact, she seemed to be with a lean aristocratic type with a deep tan and sparkling eyes. Julie looked up fetchingly into this stranger's face as she spoke to him and he bent toward her. Gerald slipped off the bar stool and hurried into the lobby, as if by accident going through the little group as the Israelites had gone through the Red Sea.

"Gerald, for heaven's sake," Julie cried. Her tone was censorious and her brow clouded.

"I'm sorry. My mind was on something else."

"Than what?" the aristocrat asked.

"Are you leaving?"

"I am." She added pointedly, "With Rolfe."

"This is Rolfe?"

Julie introduced him to her companion and to the other couples. Gerald was suddenly depressed by the realization that their circumstances prevented him from knowing any of her friends. Rolfe was with the Norwegian consulate in Chicago and in the area briefly on business.

"Julie and I were in school together," he said.

"In Norway?"

When he smiled long white teeth appeared.

"St. Olaf's."

"In Minnesota," Julie explained. Gerald knew all about her damned school. "Well, I say let's get going. I'm golfing tomorrow." And for a moment her lidded lovely eyes rested on Gerald and the gloom that had descended on him when he saw her gaze upward at this Norse god lifted.

* * *

100

"Rolfe?" Julie asked on the first tee shortly after one the following afternoon. She was taking her club back and then bringing it forward, in slow motion, over and over, limbering up. It was as if she had forgotten her escort of the night before. "I almost never see him."

"You were in school together."

"It seems so long ago."

It had been five years since Julie graduated from the liberal arts college in southern Minnesota. Her mother was Norwegian and St. Olaf's was a family tradition. Her father was the first on his side to go beyond high school.

"I was consumed with jealousy."

"You're kidding." But she smiled with unconcealed delight.

"I couldn't sleep."

"Poor Gerald."

"Don't worry about Gerald. Worry about Julie. A buck a hole."

"You're on."

He won the toss and sent his ball on an easy intentional hook two hundred and twenty-five yards on the fly. It rolled another twenty yards to precisely the spot from which he could reach the green with a five iron. Julie made a little noise, presumably complimentary, brought her club back perfectly, but on the downswing turned her knee and sent the ball skidding along the ground and into the rough seventy-five yards from the tee.

"Take a mulligan," Gerald said.

She just shook her head and began marching toward her ball. Of course, they walked and carried their clubs. Carts were for the middle-aged and out of shape. Gerald would have preferred that Julie's drive had been as good as his own. She was very competitive and fully intended to beat him, as she had on occasion in the past.

Julie's three wood out of the rough should have been caught on film. The ball rose in a slow authoritative line and because of the overspin coming out of the tall grass rolled fifty yards beyond Gerald's. His five iron was long enough but the ball refused to stay on line and rolled into a trap to the left of the green, right under a lip. Julie's seven iron put her ball within ten feet of the hole. She was whistling as she set off for the green.

The recording angel took down their strokes, hole by hole, and their guardian angels knew the war that went on within each of them. On the one hand was the desire to whip one's opponent, on the other, the more tender feelings they felt for one another and which, after all, explained their being together on this perfect July afternoon. Tension lifted on the lake hole when they both hit balls into the water.

"Should we retrieve them?"

It was a shallow, man-made lake and there was a flat-bottomed boat in which were oars and a metal cup on a long arm designed to fetch balls from the water. That boat held tender memories for the two young people. In it, more than once, they had forgotten their landbound rivalry and, spurred by the opposition to their friendship, enjoyed the stolen moments the lake hole offered. Gerald guided the boat behind a willow whose branches touched the surface of the water. When he turned to Julie shadows created by the overhanging tree flickered across her face. She lifted her face to his as she had to the Norwegian consul's the night before and he tasted the salt of his perspiration as well as her lips. She drew closer to him, although it was impossible to get into a truly comfortable position in the boat. This discomfort seemed a symbol of the moral law. Their love was ardent, even passionate, but clean as a whistle. Julie was saving herself for the man she married. Gerald intended that man to be himself, no matter the opposition to the match on Andrew's and her father's parts.

"Why didn't you show your girlfriend home last night?"

"She was with a Norwegian."

"I meant the merry widow."

"Catherine? We hardly know one another. Besides, I don't think of her that way."

"Which way?"

"Look, you brought her up. She's a client, Andrew's client."

"She's a fraud."

"We'll see."

"Do you think my father would let a client as important as Stanley Waggoner be led down the garden path by a fortune-hunting nurse?"

He ran his finger along her upper lip. "Do you really care whether or not she inherits all Stanley's money?"

"My father does."

"In his shoes, so would I. My own attention is on something entirely different, the girl who was found dead in Overlook Cemetery the day Stanley was buried."

That morning there had been a series of stories in the *Dealer* by Rebecca Prell. Pretty obviously Hanson had told her about the Bloomington flap and Rebecca had gone down there to fill out the story. Rebecca's readers could be forgiven if they thought the girl had been murdered by vengeful pornographers who had been stung by her accusations.

"What is your interest in the case?"

"I am representing the accused."

"The accused!"

"Will Foley. He was arrested last night and became our client this morning."

The insouciance with which he passed on this information to Julie did not match the alarm he had felt that morning when Andrew had responded to the call from Will Foley and almost immediately agreed to defend him.

"My associate Gerald Rowan will be principal counsel but we will work in tandem as we always do."

Will Foley looked from Andrew to Gerald and back again. "I called you because I saw you out at Overlook when the body was discovered. With the constable?"

Did Foley think Andrew was out looking for business? It was clear to Gerald during his first extensive discussion with Foley throughout the morning that Foley had no idea he had snagged the best lawyer in Wyler as his defense attorney.

"It's because she worked for Andrew this summer," Susannah said.

Helga. Gerald would have suggested this fact as a possible impediment to their defending Foley if he had really been consulted on the matter, but nothing could have overridden Andrew's predilection for lost causes. Will Foley seemed to Gerald a man who might be feeling remorse, but not one who was innocent of the charges.

"I wouldn't have raised a hand to that girl."

"Never hit a woman?"

Foley ducked his head. There were those who had told the

sheriff that Foley abused his wife. In the classic manner of domestic disputes, once the spouses were reconciled they resented being reminded of the fact that the wife had felt it necessary to call the police to protect her against her husband. Now the police were intrusive busybodies. Clearly, Foley's defense could not be his courtly manner with women in general.

Foley had the weatherworn look of a man who worked outdoors. His beard had red streaks, his eyes were in a perpetual squint and when he relaxed his forehead was streaked with white unsunburnt wrinkle lines.

"I didn't kill her."

That was the assumption on which Gerald would proceed, no matter his personal doubts on the subject. But that first interview made it even more difficult to believe that Will Foley was innocent.

"Let's try to get clear about your car first. The body was found in a car registered in your name."

"It was stolen."

"When did you report it?"

"I didn't realize it until I saw it parked out there with Helga in it."

"So you reported the theft of your car after you discovered the body in it."

"That sounds bad, doesn't it?"

"The main thing now is to get everything laid out as clearly as we can so we know how to proceed." You didn't have to be a lawyer to imagine what the prosecution would do with Foley's stolen vehicle.

"The pickup you drove from home was parked in your driveway."

"That's right."

"And the garage door was shut?"

"You leave a garage door open in that neighborhood and people just help themselves. It was shut. I'm surprised they didn't take the pickup too. I put the keys above the sun visor. You gotta realize I don't really wake up until I get to the maintenance shed and have a cup of coffee."

"You don't have breakfast at home?"

"The reason I wear a beard? I rinse my face going through the kitchen, get behind that wheel and drive to work like a robot."

"What time you leave?"

"The alarm goes off at six-fifteen."

"Your wife get up then too?"

His wife slept in, no need for her to get up that early. Even if he had eaten breakfast at home, toast and coffee would have been enough, or doughnuts—even simpler, a glass of juice—and that would be it. No point in his wife getting up to fix a breakfast like that.

"But she would know when you left the house."

"Of course she would."

"You sleep together?"

He obviously wanted to lie. One of her grievances was the way he sprawled while he slept. He would whip out an arm and she could be clobbered at any moment. She wasn't always that sure he was really asleep when this happened. She had set up a single bed in the boys' room. Gerald did not feel that he was getting a peek into an ideal marriage.

He envied the prosecutor the case he would have. A body is found in Foley's car and then he decides to report it stolen. There were rumors around Overlook that he had pursued Helga when she worked at the cemetery the summer before, and apparently they had gone out a few times. The wandering husband's home life would not suggest any deterrent to such fooling around. Gerald did not like the thought that he had succeeded Will Foley as Helga's escort. He got back to the car.

"Let me tell you what the prosecutor is going to think and you tell me what's wrong with it."

Foley hunched forward as if he were about to take a test.

"He'll say, Look, we don't even know for sure that this guy was home the night before. If his wife says he was, under questioning it will emerge that they slept in separate rooms, she didn't get up when he left in the morning, he might never have been there and she wouldn't know the difference."

"That's nuts."

"Why?"

" 'Cause I was there."

"Of course, you were there. Of course, you got up when you said and drove to work in your pickup. But the prosecutor is going to question that. How can we show him he's nuts?"

"He's going to say I killed her and left her in my car and then went home for my pickup, drove to work and told everybody there's a car parked out in Resurrection? Why wouldn't I just report the car missing?"

Gerald nodded, as if Foley had made a good point. Of course, the prosecutor would remind him that he didn't know his car was stolen.

"This guy think I'm some dumb son of a bitch? The way you put it, I'd have to be nuts. Why leave her in the car at all?"

Andrew had come in for the last part of this and he provided the answer to Foley's question.

"To frame you, Foley. What else?"

Andrew seemed to be serious.

Andrew met Hanson for lunch in the café off the lobby of the courthouse. Tuna salad on lettuce, iced tea, lots of soda crackers.

"Gerald will be principal defender of Foley," he told Hanson.

"You think Foley did it?"

"We're pleading him innocent."

"Is that your answer?"

Andrew smiled. "I only defend the innocent. While I'm defending them, and until and unless they're proved guilty, they are innocent."

"It looks bad."

"You think he did it?"

"No."

Andrew looked at Hanson, an experienced, sensible investigator, a man with whom he had worked in the past and respected greatly. But Andrew knew that the stuff in the paper about pornography in Bloomington had to be due to a lead from Hanson. Helga's mother had chased the reporter Rebecca Prell from the yard with a BB gun when she had tried to talk with the older woman about her daughter's film career at college.

"Andrew, Will Foley is dumb, but how dumb? If he were dumb enough to kill the girl he would have just killed her. But to kill her and leave her in his own car and stage a discovery of the body and then report his car stolen after the fact makes no sense."

"What does make sense?"

"He's been set up. His car is stolen, the girl is killed and left in Foley's car and he leads everybody to it. Hey, that's my car. Someone must have stolen it. He looks guilty as sin."

"He does."

"The only question is, who set him up?"

Hanson sat back and tipped his head so he could look at the ceiling. He lowered his chin until his eyes met Andrew's.

"How much do you know about her filming in Bloomington?"

"Only what I read in the paper. And what you told me."

"That's just the tip of the iceberg. Andrew, pornography has been big business for a long time, but it is booming like never before. Now you don't have to go to some sleazy theater or bookstore, you rent a video or you tap into it on the worldwide web. The demand for materials is enormous. CD-ROMs are flourishing, but the technology does not stand still. Accessibility is no longer a problem; non-accessibility is, and

the courts have thrown up their hands. You can't police something this global and amorphous. What has to be localized is
the production of the crud. It is very easy to produce stuff of
the quality necessary for the trade. People learn the game
working for a crew and then set up on their own and make
their own films."

"And Helga got caught up in that in Bloomington?"

"Half innocently, say, but enough to be compromised. The
editing of the film put her right in the midst of the raunchiest
scenes."

"Have you seen the result?"

"A CD version was mailed to Mrs. Bjornsen. She didn't
know what the hell it was and had no computer to view it
on. But Helga got the message."

"Which was?"

"Play ball or you're disgraced."

"You mean play ball or you're dead?"

Hanson nodded. It was a theory with its attractions. It
moved the center of gravity of the murder out of Wyler. But
it was clear that Hanson was only guessing.

"Do you have anything concrete tying her murder to the
bunch in Bloomington?"

"No."

"Do you think that can be done?"

"It's the only hope."

"That isn't the way the prosecutor will see it. What you
propose has no evidence for it and it sets aside evidence already
had. The theft of the vehicle, for example. He can tie that to
Foley. At least he reasonably thinks he can. There is the reality
of Foley's car."

"I know, I know."

"And why would they have decided on Foley? How would they even know about him?"

"Helga went out with him a couple of times last summer."

Andrew sat in silence. She might have mentioned that to a friend, in confidence, the wrong friend, and provided her eventual enemies with a tie they needed in her hometown.

Rebecca had been convinced of the plausibility of Hanson's theory from the time she first heard it, and her trip to Bloomington had made it more promising. She spoke with a girl Helga had roomed with, Shirley Plotnik, a short blonde with a worried expression.

"There were three of us, but I moved out. It wasn't Helga, it was Mimi Mannheim I didn't like. And she had this influence over Helga. More and more I was excluded and afterward when Helga and I talked, well, was I glad I hadn't made the grade with Mimi."

Mimi was the recruiter of coeds for Reality Productions, and she began by checking out the girls who signed up for the photography course taught by a man named Fodor. A come-on was the promise of a shot at commercial modeling. Getting a girl before a camera, still or movie, was the essential first step.

"How can I get in touch with Mimi?"

"Oh, she left with Fodor and the rest of them. It looks like they don't stay in the same place for long."

It was only after Rebecca read her own story in print that she realized, if the pornography angle was the solution to Helga's murder, then the murder was insoluble. Tracking down the filming crew would require a full court press and it was pretty clear that Hanson was detailed to Wyler for a finite period of time and for a very specific purpose. He would be reassigned before he could even get a start on locating Fodor, let alone link him to the brutal murder of Helga.

Rebecca drove to Overlook, parked behind the office and changed into running shoes. She set off up the road toward the spot where the body of Helga had been found. The rhythm of running made thinking episodic but she had come here to jog away her skepticism about the Bloomington connection. Talking with Shirley Plotnik about Mimi and of what Helga had done on campus seemed impossibly remote from this cemetery where the body had been found.

The road rose and she began to feel the strain on her calves but concentrated on her running, thereby interrupting whatever line of thought had begun. Overlook was a peaceful place, especially here in the older sections where the dead had been lying for a century and more and the terrain was no longer disturbed by the digging of new graves. The crew kept the lawns mowed, trimming the grass around the markers with a hand-held gadget that whirled a length of wire that scythed through the grass. One of Helga's jobs had been to water the permanent flowers that had been planted in tubs and hanging pots. Rebecca was resolved to do a piece on local cemeteries. The price of a lot bought years and years of care costing far more than anyone originally paid.

"How do you make any money?" she had asked Gladys.

"Who says we make any money?"

"But there are all these people working here, the upkeep, all the rest."

"How many plots you think we have here?"

"I could only make a wild guess."

"Well, multiply that by, say, five hundred dollars and see what you get. Add the charge for digging the grave and attendant services."

"I'll have to think about it."

Above and beyond the monetary side of it, Rebecca was trying to get a sense of the kind of person who went off each morning to work in a cemetery. Gladys, of course, could pretend that she was working in just any office. As for Schmucker, he had inherited the place, so what further excuse did he need? Gladys said he spent all day in his office surfing the web and that seemed to be true. Every time Rebecca had been in the Overlook office the door of the sexton's office had been closed and the blinds of the intervening window had been drawn.

Rebecca had some acquaintance with the worldwide web, but she had never been willing to sit down and spend hours chasing from one site to another. When she returned from her jog, she stepped into the office, welcoming the air-conditioning. Gladys looked up.

"I thought that was you who ran by."

"Isn't he here?" The sexton's door was open.

"Wednesday afternoon he takes off."

Rebecca opened the door and looked in. One wall of the

sexton's office was a picture window but it was closed off by the pulled blinds. There was a large desk with several chairs facing it and behind it a huge comfortable chair facing the computer. Rebecca looked at Gladys, nodded at the empty office and lifted her brows.

"Go ahead."

The computer was on. Rebecca sat and looked at the squirmy screen saver that writhed across the monitor, changing colors as it did so. She hit the space bar and Yahoo, a favorite search engine for negotiating the web, became visible. Rebecca trolled down the screen and noticed the different colors of the words designating categories. A darker color indicated that the word had been clicked on. Obviously, Schmucker had checked out the Computer category. She clicked on it and was given a menu. The color of Search Engines indicated that Schmucker had clicked it; Rebecca did the same, and there was a list of engines. She trolled down. Several had been used by Schmucker. And then she came to Naughty. When she clicked on it she found herself on the threshold of computer porn. She realized that Gladys was standing beside her.

"You really know how to use that, don't you?"

"I was tracking a route Schmucker has taken. Can you read that screen?"

Gladys bent forward and squinted, moving her lips as she read. She straightened up and looked at Rebecca. "Sounds pretty wild."

"Pick one."

Gladys pointed, Rebecca clicked, and a screen asked her to indicate that she was eighteen or older. She clicked and suddenly on the screen were pictures to rival those on the covers of girlie magazines.

"Wow. No wonder he's at it all day."

Rebecca backed up until she was back on the Yahoo home page. She got out of that and went back to Windows 95. Rows of icons were on the left of the screen, permitting easy access. Nothing surprising there. Rebecca dropped the cursor to Start, then ran it up to programs and checked out what Schmucker had. Coed Lust caught her eye. She activated it. On the screen appeared a number of pictures of nude women, alone and together, and Rebecca was instructed to insert the appropriate CD in the D drive.

"That's Helga," Gladys said in hushed tones, pointing to one of the pictures. "My God, that's Helga."

Rebecca spoke to Regina Foote about Will Foley. Did she think he could have killed Helga?

"He's a ladykiller, but not in that sense. Actually, he is a gentle man."

"He certainly doesn't seem to be a murderer," Rebecca said, if only to keep the conversation going.

"He's like a little boy. Most men are."

She had very long artificial nails that gave her trouble when she tried to pry a cigarette from a new pack. She got it lit and then propped an elbow in her lap, held a hand before her face, and exhaled a roomful of smoke.

"Want one?"

"Not now."

Not ever. Rebecca had never even tried cigarettes. She would rather ask for condoms than cigarettes in a drugstore, but she had never done that either.

Fiona Foley had suggested that Rebecca talk to Regina.

"What would she know?"

But it seemed that Mrs. Foley's main interest was to get rid of Rebecca. It was hard to tell what the woman thought of her husband's predicament. Her kids were raising all kinds of hell in the next room, fighting over the remote control, but she just tuned them out. She hadn't read the stories in the paper; she never read the paper. Local news? The kids had a program on at that time on one of the cable channels.

"Did you hear your husband leave for work that morning?"

"I never hear him. He goes very early."

"What would you say if the prosecutor claimed that Will had not been home that night, that he wasn't here to leave for work?"

She shrugged.

The face of Sonny Apple seemed turned brightly toward the future, the yet to be, the promise of tomorrow, but this was deceptive. At thirty-eight, Sonny was disappointed in what he had already seen of tomorrow, and his faith that better was on the way was waning. His job was not without its compensations, but it was a dead end. It was difficult to think of director of public relations in the Schaumberg Public Library as a big item on his résumé. The pay was good; in fact, that was one of the problems—it was too good. This library system was the beneficiary of a phenomenal tax base because the suburb west of Chicago was in metastasis, new businesses settling there by the dozens every month. Nearby suburbs were more residential. Schaumberg had never met a business it didn't like and the chamber of commerce and city council went a long way toward making relocation attractive. Sonny doubted that he could match his salary in any other library system in the country.

"We are in thrall to affluence," he said in the staff lounge, uncrossing his long legs and then recrossing them the other way.

"You got that release for the visiting authors series ready, Sonny?"

He smiled at Mrs. Wiggins. "You haven't heard a word I said."

"That's because you never stop talking."

"Librarians are supposed to talk on break. To make up for the silence." But silence was no longer obligatory in the library. Whispering was encouraged, but many spoke in a normal tone of voice. Sonny had been shocked by this at first, as he might have been by people talking in church.

Mae Wiggins was fond of saying that the facilities of the Schaumberg library rivaled those of many research libraries at universities. An exaggeration, perhaps, but it gave some sense of what money could buy. The services offered to local businesses were many and various; there were self-help classes and other activities only dubiously related to books. But then books were only one of the things libraries now provided. Videos had been very big for a long time, but now rental fees were low and copies of films so reasonable that this service had obviously crested, much to Mae's consternation. The administrative ideal was to increase the budget each year, not turn back unspent portions of what had already been allotted them.

It was at this dark moment that Sonny had been inspired. "Genealogy," he said.

There was a delayed reaction. Mae turned. "What did you say?"

"Genealogy."

This had become his passion ever since he'd attended a very pedestrian talk on the subject the previous year. The computer system at the library enabled him to tap into databases around the country, around the world, and soon the lure of the past had captivated him. It became Sonny's passion to discover his origins.

There was, he supposed, some correlation between the mobility and rootlessness of the country and a desire to find stability in one's ancestors. Schaumberg and the area around it seemed a metaphor of the split. On the one hand, acres of spanking new buildings that had not been so much as a twinkle in an architect's eye a decade ago, on the other, beyond, the fields where corn and soybeans still grew, as they had grown a few years earlier, where suburban buildings now stood. The land represented the past, stability, the rich loam out of which they all had come.

"What about genealogy?" Mae asked.

It seemed even more of an inspiration as he spoke. There would be a bank of computers dedicated to the use of those patrons who wished to look into their family trees. There would be a series of lectures on genealogy, the sources, the means, the computer programs, the whole bit. There would be a consultant on duty at all times.

"Who?"

"You will have to hire someone."

So it was that Cynthia Thanos joined the staff of the library. Mae Wiggins was quite explicit in letting Cynthia know that she owed her employment to the brainstorm of Sonny Apple.

"We're lucky to have you," he said, taking in the great mane of hair, the olive skin, the wide generous mouth, the earth mother body. He knew from her application that she was thirty-four but wondered what he would have guessed without that knowledge. Ageless, he decided. There was something mystical about Cynthia.

"First generation," she answered in reply to his question as to how long her family had been in America. "My father has gone back to Greece. Greeks love to retire to Athens."

It struck Sonny that her blood could be traced back to pre-Christian times, to the days of the Peloponnesian War. When he eventually said this to her, she smiled.

"My blood is no older than anyone else's."

The difference lay in having an idea where one's remote forebears had lived. Sonny Apple had only the vaguest notion of the origin of his grandparents. He had learned that he was connected with the Waggoner family that had prospered in a small Indiana town during the early days of the automobile and then apparently faded into oblivion.

Cynthia was not impressed by this, nor was she interested in such recent linkages. Her passion was to drive bloodlines back into the eighteenth, the seventeenth, the sixteenth century and beyond.

"Of course, the records prevent this, by and large. Not everyone merited attention from chroniclers and clerks. But the recent development of popular history is opening up the peasantry of the Middle Ages to us as never before."

Cynthia's mother had been Irish and this complicated her pursuit because the British had been such bastards in Ireland.

"Do you know Trollope's Irish novels?"

Cynthia just looked at him.

"Trollope married an Irishwoman."

"Probably Anglo-Irish." Cynthia made as if to spit. "That is what my mother would do."

Cynthia and her program were an enormous hit. There was a backlist of applicants for her course, as the series of six talks was billed by Sonny. Graduates of the course sat for hours at the dedicated computers and Mae Wiggins added more. She was ecstatic. Not only was the program popular, it was expensive.

Sonny felt released to pursue the spoor of the Waggoner connection. Soon he was in touch with half a dozen shirttail relatives. He drove over to Wyler to talk to Jeb Riverside, who was a cousin at three removes.

Jeb Riverside had known of Sonny Apple before Sonny contacted him. Jeb had a pretty complete list of possible claimants to the Waggoner fortune, but unlike Sonny he thought this was information to keep confidential.

"How many slices in a pie?" he asked Sonny the first time they met. They were at the counter in the Tippecanoe Truck Stop having lemon meringue pie and a mug of the coffee the drivers called "number 30 oil."

"I don't understand."

"What we are is heirs, Sonny. Now, the more heirs, the less pie, right?"

The librarian's response was not encouraging. Jeb had assumed Sonny would understand that they didn't want to beat the bushes to find even more people with half a claim to the Waggoner money.

"I thought Waggoner went bust."

"The automobile manufacturing did. It's old Stanley who makes the thing worthwhile."

He told Sonny of the scion of the house of Waggoner who had taken the little he had been given and by wise and diversified investments turned it into a very impressive amount of money. Even as he spoke, he wondered if he shouldn't have sent this lanky librarian back to Schaumberg without telling him anything about Stanley's money. He had assumed that Sonny already knew about it. He had assumed that was why Sonny was paying this visit. He had already made an appointment with Frank McGough so Sonny could meet him. Lars could look after the driving range while he was downtown.

"My God, another one," McGough said.

Jeb hadn't told McGough that there could be double the number if other Waggoner connections realized their status. "I wanted him to meet you and find out what you've done for us."

McGough liked to dramatize his first meeting with Stanley Waggoner, talking as if he had overcome the old man's reluctance to acknowledge his blood relatives by eloquence and rhetoric, but the meetings Jeb had sat in on went as smooth as silk. Stanley showed interest in understanding exactly what the connection was between Jeb and the Waggoners. Halfway through Jeb's account the old man began to smile.

"I suppose we're all related one way or the other."

Well, if the direct heir of the Waggoner money could be linked to Jeb, who had Indian blood in him, and the Indians had indeed come across the Bering Strait from Asia, some going down into Mexico and starting Mayan civilization, others fanning out over the North American continent, the old man was probably right.

"Adam and Eve."

"Exactly."

The main thing was his being well disposed to the arrangements worked out with McGough. The one thing the old man resisted was the suggestion that these matters be taken care of while he was still alive.

"I would feel as if I had already died. No, let's wait until I am gone."

McGough was inclined to press the matter, but Jeb stopped him. He was the designated representative of the claimants and he did not want the old man to get his back up now.

Jeb persuaded Sonny to get the Waggoner genealogy off the personal page he had on the web. Anyone could read it and even download it. Jeb himself downloaded it before he had Sonny delete it.

"I think I'll check out my mother's side," Sonny said. "Maybe I'll strike oil there too."

Frank McGough was a good advocate and there was no need to explain to him that they had all the claimants they needed already. Even so, the lawyer had pulled a long face when he showed Jeb the obituary of one of the claimants from the Detroit paper.

"How did you find that?"

It seemed that there was a database of obituaries, a convenience for estate lawyers and the like. They preferred learning for themselves when a client had died and it was time to execute the will.

"There's no mention of any Waggoner connection," McGough observed.

Of course, anyone who knew of the amount of money that would be distributed on the death of Stanley Waggoner became very sensitive to the possibility that the mere mention of the name would bring more claimants out of the woodwork.

"How old was he?" Jeb asked of the deceased Detroit claimant.

"Just fifty-seven."

"Heart attack?"

McGough shook his head. "The obituary doesn't say this but I had a paralegal get a copy of the issues of the paper on this and preceding days. The poor guy was nailed by a hit-and-run driver."

Jeb shook his head at the senselessness of things. "That close to becoming rich and he gets run over."

"Take care of yourself," McGough said.

The remark stayed with Jeb afterward and he turned it over and over in his mind, wondering what the lawyer had meant. McGough was someone you had to be always on your guard with, never relax. He was a hardball pitcher if ever there was one.

23

The driving range had been located on the county highway west of town forever. As a kid, Andrew had stopped there from time to time to shoot a bucket of balls, enjoying the ohs and ahs as he sailed them out there. In those days the range had been operated by a one-armed man named Lefty who could whack a ball two hundred yards with his one arm. It was still called Lefty's Hook.

Andrew got a pail of balls and placed one on the nipplelike tee emerging from the rubber matted surface. He looked up the line where three kids were spraying balls all over the place. They seemed to think the point was to hit as many balls as possible in as short a time as possible. Behind Andrew, there would be a swoosh, the crack of club on ball, followed by profanity. Andrew addressed his ball, swung easily and laid it out to the two-hundred-and-fifty-yard marker. The second time he did it the man behind him said, "Jesus."

Andrew turned and watched the fellow slice a couple of balls. "Slow down," Andrew advised. "And bring your right foot forward a little."

The man followed these admonitions and hit an adequate drive. Then he hit another. His face was wreathed in smiles when he looked at Andrew. Andrew left him to his temporary bliss. Tomorrow—at any rate, soon—some other glitch would show up in the man's game and he would be swearing again.

"You Jeb Riverside?" he asked the man behind the counter. He already knew that he was. The man seemed unsure. Andrew showed him a card. "Frank McGough would advise you not to talk to me."

"He already has." He turned to the sunburnt man who sat reading a magazine. "Lars, leave us alone for a minute."

"He work here?" Andrew asked after the man shuffled silently out.

"As little as possible."

"Did you recognize me?"

"As soon as you hit those balls."

"You do understand that nothing my client gains in any way affects your fortunes?"

"McGough says she would become executor."

"That doesn't mean she can change the will."

"Why are you telling me this?"

"So you won't misunderstand why McGough and I are engaged in all-out war. He is after me and I am after him. It's a long story. Just don't think it jeopardizes you."

"I appreciate your concern."

"How are you related to the Waggoners?"

"The wrong side of the blanket."

"Then I *could* do you harm if I wanted to."

Riverside tried a carefree smile. "No. We have formed a legal corporation and I am as much a member as the others."

"But one of them could contest your right to inherit."

"We've been through all that. Stanley Waggoner acknowledged me as an heir."

"That ought to do it."

"That was pretty good advice you gave that duffer."

"Let me give you some advice. Keep an eye on Frank McGough."

McGough was intent on quashing Catherine's claim because after he had satisfied Jeb Riverside and the legal grouping he had formed of Waggoner claimants, there would still remain the administration of the many charitable and educational trusts that Waggoner had set up, as well as the not-for-profit foundation with an endowment of twenty-five million meant to further the education of the descendants of Waggoner employees. Managing all that capital would mean lots of money even for an honest manager, but for Frank McGough it would represent an irresistible temptation.

Rebecca Prell stopped by to get information about the challenge of the Waggoner will. "Foster thinks it might have some local interest."

"What sort of information would you like?" Andrew asked.

"You're representing the woman who married Stanley Waggoner in the nursing home, right?"

"Mrs. Waggoner is my client, yes."

"And she poses a threat to the other heirs? The blood re-lations?"

"I think we'd better start at the beginning."

He gave her an inkling of what the Waggoner Corporation had once meant to Wyler and what a devastating thing its demise had been. Not that there had been a lack of consideration for employees, but some fateful decisions had been made from which there was no going back. The Waggoners were not prolific breeders. Once a son was born and the succession assured, they seemed to feel they had done their duty to the family and to the race. No provision had been made for a Stanley, who went childless and brideless into old age.

"He waited too long to have children, didn't he?"

"I don't think that was his intention when he married Catherine."

"Has she left town? I'd love to interview her."

"I'll arrange it." He paused, hoping she would see this as a quid pro quo. "A story on the group of presumed heirs that has been formed and which was recognized by Stanley himself would also be interesting."

"How many are there?"

"I would start with Jeb Riverside, right here in Wyler."

24

"Why do you drive such a toy?" Cynthia Thanos said when she asked Sonny for a lift home one night early in her employment in Schaumberg.

"This is the kind of car I rent in Europe."

"Is that your answer?"

"The fact is, I drive greater distances there than here. My apartment is half a mile from work."

"Let me see it."

"Sure. When?"

"Now?"

Sonny's smile did not waver. What was Cynthia up to? Had this been the reason behind asking him for a ride home? In a way yes, and innocently so.

"I am being pressured by the realtor. I want to get out of the Holiday Inn but I don't want to pick an apartment hastily."

"I'm content with mine."

The development was across I-90, toward Barrington, straddling a gulchlike valley with a lively but narrow creek burbling through it. The buildings were built on the inclines of either bank, the trees on the property were full growth, there was no maintenance or gardening, yet the apartments were not condominiums. Villagio Sopra Acqua. Cynthia liked the name right off.

He unlocked the door and let her go first. She strode across the kitchen and stood in the two-story living area and looked at the loftlike area above where the two bedrooms were.

"Two bedrooms!"

"One is my study."

His tone as he said this was all wrong, as if he were fending off her suggestion that she move in with him. He had been trying to have nothing but professional thoughts about Cynthia, particularly since she persisted in seeing him as her champion.

"Mae told me," she would say, waving away his protests. "My job was all your idea."

"Well, you've certainly made it work."

Her eyes looked deeply into his. "I see this as an opportunity of a lifetime. Do you know what I was earning before I came here?"

Actually he did. Applications provided reminders to those involved in hiring that they lived in an economically unreal world.

"May I?" she asked, indicating the stairs to the loft.

"Go ahead."

He stayed below, opened a beer, got out some cheese and crackers. "I have some retsina," he called to Cynthia.

"Yes, thank you. This is marvelous!"

They sat out on the porch and listened to the water below and the muted roar from I-90. Cynthia was enthralled. The upshot was that they called the office and the manager agreed to come back at seven-thirty and show Cynthia an apartment that would be available at the beginning of the month.

"If it's like this, I will take it."

"They're all alike, really."

She had noticed his computer upstairs. With a modem he could call into the library computer and surf the web at the taxpayes' expense. She drank half the bottle of retsina and said she would finish it after her appointment with the manager. At a quarter of eight she was helloing him from a balcony across the creek. She took the apartment. They went out to dinner; afterward she wanted to see her apartment again, if only from his balcony, and she finished the retsina and he opened another. Actually, he had been thinking of her when he bought it. He himself didn't much care for it.

At eleven he took her to the Holiday Inn. "Will your car be working tomorrow?"

"There's nothing wrong with my car."

Then why had she taken a cab to work that morning? He took the minor mystery home with him. What would it be like to have Cynthia in an apartment just across the creek from his? Belatedly it occurred to him that it would be like taking his work home with him.

A man does not arrive at the age of thirty-eight still a bachelor by inadvertence. Until he was thirty, Sonny always imagined that he would get married someday, even soon, and it added zest to the single life. After thirty he began to think he would need reasons to alter his status. The realization that he would be thought to be marrying late, that his children would be toddlers when his contemporaries had kids in high school, that little and large routines would have to be changed with marriage, did not amount to an argument, but an indisposition to marry set in. He did not like to examine it, because it had its selfish aspect. A wife and children would be disruptive factors in his life, whatever consolations they undoubtedly represented. He told himself that if he reached forty still single that would seal it. He would be a bachelor forever.

"You're not married," Cynthia said. They were on her balcony, from which he got an angled view of his own.

"No."

"Have you been?"

"Have you?"

"Yes."

"What happened?"

"He died."

"I'm sorry."

"It was a terrible blow. However, he was twenty years my senior so it was not completely a surprise."

Sonny waited. If she wanted to go on he would listen but he found he did not want to know these things about Cynthia. He wanted to encourage in her the notion that relocating to Schaumberg began an entirely new chapter in her life. Like Villagio Sopra Acqua, everything was new.

He told her of his amateurish plunge into genealogy. He had been raised half a continent away and found himself bereft of parents before he was twenty, an only son who now seemed the solitary Apple on his branch of the family tree. One unbusy day at the Schaumberg library he had put a toe tentatively into the waters out of which he had emerged.

"And what did you find?"

"I have a correspondent who insists that he and I and a few others are legitimate heirs of the Waggoner fortune. He reminded me of the Duke of Bilgewater."

She frowned in incomprehension.

"Huckleberry Finn."

She still did not understand. He realized that there was a whole world of books not yet open to Cynthia. It seemed fitting that he should transmit to her his enthusiasm for fiction in return for what he learned from her about genealogy. She checked out Jeb Riverside's claim.

"He's right. Is there a Waggoner fortune?"

"I have no idea."

"Haven't you looked into it?"

That he might come into a large amount of money seemed a thought on a par with winning the lottery. Cynthia looked at him in wonder and then drew him into a plush embrace. "You're marvelous."

Their friendship deepened but remained Platonic, which seemed to be what they both wanted. Affection was expressed by kisses on the cheek, an infrequent embrace, but these were gestures extended to many others and carried no special significance. It was the accident that transposed their relationship into another key.

They drove separately to the library and separately back again at night. They had never discussed carpooling. Each morning, Sonny would go down the stairs to the lot and get behind the wheel of his miniature automobile with wheels the size of a tractor lawn mower's and head down the service road to the bridge that would carry him across I-90 to Schaumberg. It happened just as he was leaving the bridge. He felt a jolt, the angle of the car tipped steeply and he saw one of his wheels roll on ahead. Meanwhile his axle was giving off a horrendous noise as well as sparks as it dragged along the concrete, and then he lost control. The last thing he saw was the grill of the car he was about to hit head-on.

The first thing he saw when he came to was Cynthia. She was not looking at him; her expression was sad, even tragic, and his hand, he realized, was held tightly in hers.

"I'm alive."

She turned to him, gave out a little cry, and then her face descended to his and her hair engulfed them as she pressed her mouth to his. There was no point in embracing him, given the body cast that extended downward to his hips. An ankle too, had been broken. There wasn't a scratch on his face. Cynthia rained kisses on him as if to prove it.

"It's a miracle you're alive."

"What happened?"

For that, she ceded her place to a stumpy man with thin hair that rose in an unconvincing crew cut. He looked to be in his forties.

"Who would want to kill you?"

"I don't understand the question."

"Someone sawed halfway through your axle and fooled with the steering mechanism. You were an accident waiting to happen."

"My car was fixed to crash?"

"No doubt about it."

"I have no enemies." He really believed this, but it did sound hubristic, as if he were claiming that everyone loved him, but logically that was quite another claim. Who could wish him harm? He honestly could think of no one.

Meanwhile, Inspector Dumke interviewed Sonny's colleagues at the library and word got out that he was looking for someone who wished Sonny Apple was dead. Mae called a halt to this, insisting that Sonny was the most beloved member of her staff. He was a threat to no one, a help to all, a joy to work with. Tears welled in her eyes during this testimonial.

Dumke turned his curiosity to Cynthia.

"He wants to know where my husband lives."

"Isn't he dead?"

She nodded. "I told him Hades and he wanted to know what state that is in."

"What did you tell him?"

"Indiana."

Her Greek Orthodox faith was another vast area of unfamiliarity to him. He knew little to nothing of organized religion. Or disorganized.

"You're a pagan," she observed.

"Wasn't everybody once?"

While he mended, they talked of many things. She took him home to her apartment and it was like being in his own, more or less. As the weeks passed his own place across the creek seemed redundant. Jeb Riverside telephoned and Cynthia told him of the accident in some detail. The next day flowers and a box of peanut brittle for "Cousin Jonathan" arrived at Sonny's address.

"Jonathan?"

"It's my name."

"I prefer Sonny."

"So do I."

A day before they had agreed he could move back into his own apartment and fend for himself, they looked across the creek and saw flames leaping from the doors leading out to his balcony. The place was gutted by the fire but the loft area was spared. Cynthia arranged to have his books and computer moved to her place.

"I didn't set your place on fire," she said softly. They were side by side on a sofa watching the sun descend into the west, a cosmic fire writing finis to the day he had been burned out.

"Why would you?"

"To keep you here."

They looked deeply into one another's eyes and he folded her into his arms, mindful of his still-mending chest; their kiss was a chaste promise of permanency.

The fire was ruled arson. Dumke came back. "They're still after you."

"I've moved."

The detective glanced at Cynthia. "Here?"

"We're going to get married."

"Maybe you should take her name."

"Ho ho."

Cynthia grew pensive after Dumke was gone. "He's right, you know. First your car, now your apartment."

"So what should I do?"

"We will be vigilant."

Darlene Bjornsen's notion of happiness had shrunk to a bottle of aquavit, a good movie video to drink it with and then the oblivion of sleep. She was weak but wise enough to know that such a routine, if it became daily, would lose its power to provide the relief she sought—relief from being herself, from being aware of her surroundings, from thinking about Helga.

"Your daughter is dead."

A series of strangers had come to tell her this and it was all she could do not to say that Helga had died years ago when Darlene had let slip a remark she could not call back and Helga pursued it relentlessly.

"You're not adopted, Helga."

"What do you mean?"

"You are my daughter."

"Your adopted daughter."

"Sweetheart, look at you, look at me. We are mother and daughter."

Helga had been a senior in high school then, she had been pursued by a nice boy but she held herself aloof.

"You have to tell me where I came from," she had demanded.

"Did he ask you that?"

"*I'm* asking. I can find out, you know. These things can't be kept secret anymore."

Had Helga been brooding about this? They had never discussed the matter before, but then they talked so little. Darlene had been provided for, there was no need for her to work, and over the years she had become a recluse. She shuddered at a knock on the door; she shopped late at night, when she was less likely to run into anyone who had known her.

Helga had gone downtown to the courthouse and checked the record. She found that Darlene Bjornsen had adopted baby girl Helga eighteen years before. What she could not find was any reference to the mother of the baby. And that is when Darlene had told her she was not adopted.

Helga thought she was drunk, or losing her mind, or both. The adoption was recorded at the courthouse, she had seen the entry. Of course she had. That had been part of the arrangement, an elaborate ruse to make Darlene sound noble, taking on a child. But it had been her own child, and the effort had been meant to shelter the father of the baby. The family had conducted the negotiations; Darlene had not spoken to her lover once during this time, or indeed afterward. They had sent him off to Europe.

He had not known what was going on. The lies his family had told him in order to pry him loose and send him on his way were awful. But eventually he learned the truth. A dying sister had told him everything, and he had come to visit Darlene. They looked at one another across the lost years but there was no remedy for what had been done. She could not discover in this already elderly man the imposing figure that had caused her heart to melt when she was a girl. And what he must have seen was a recluse, a woman with the telltale signs of the secret drinker.

"Is there any way I could meet her?"

"And tell her you are her father?"

"If you think I should."

Putting the decision to her might have been cunning, but she could not believe that of him. He was what he seemed, a wealthy man suddenly confronted with a past injustice in which he was implicated.

"No. She thinks she is adopted."

Helga came in while he was still there and Darlene watched the father look wondrously at his daughter. Of course, Helga had no sense of who he was or what his relationship to her was. Darlene had been certain that Stanley would burst out with the great revelation, but he did not. He was awkward with Helga. And then she was out of the room. He looked at her abjectly.

"You're right. I'll leave well enough alone."

He was solicitous about her. He wanted to move her to a better house. He promised that he would provide for Helga. Perhaps if he had come ten years before, or even five . . .

Years later when she said to Helga that she was not adopted, she had wanted to say more, but her daughter's dismissal of her great revelation deflated her. Helga returned from down-town, convinced that Darlene had lied to her, demanding to know who her true parents were.

"You met your father once."

"When? Where?"

"Here. In this room. You came home from school and he was here and I introduced you."

"Why had he come?"

"He wanted to see me. And you."

"What was his name?"

But Darlene was weary of these dramatics. Talking with Stanley had convinced her that the past was irrevocably past. He seemed no more real than Mark Larson, to whom she had been married less than a year. When he left she dropped his name. Helga might imagine that knowing who her father was would open a course of action that would change her life. But Stanley had not called again, nor had he contacted Darlene. His visit had been a self-contained episode. Perhaps he had expected something extraordinary to result from seeing her again, but they had just been a man and woman in a shadowy room who did not really know one another.

It was later that Helga, looking at some old photographs, said softly. "I do look like you."

"Yes."

Obviously, Helga had been turning over the possibility that the woman she had thought of as her foster mother was her birth mother. What change should that have effected between them?

"It could be proved."

"How?"

"With blood. DNA."

142

"You don't really want to know, Helga."

Not just then she didn't but eventually she had to know. She drew blood from Darlene's pricked finger and took the slide to the lab. It was not a standard test, but Helga had a friend whose father did tests in paternity cases. Maternity cases were all but nonexistent for obvious reasons, but the test would tell Helga if she had indeed been formed in the womb of Darlene Bjornsen.

One morning Darlene got up and Helga was waiting for her, seated at the kitchen table, coffee ready.

"It's true."

Darlene waited. She herself had not needed proof and she could not tell what this turn of events meant for Helga.

"Now all I need is my father's name."

"He is an old man now. He was much older than I."

"But he is still alive?"

"As far as I know."

That Darlene should be so disinterested in the man who was Helga's father irked her daughter. "Who is he?"

"Stanley Waggoner."

That was that. Just knowing seemed enough for Helga. But they had grown closer then, mother and child, and it had been painful for Darlene when Helga went back to Bloomington. They had had so little time to enjoy their true relationship, and now Helga was gone forever.

Her cousin Amity came back and insisted on preparing meals and sharing them with Darlene. Her husband came too but all he wanted to do was watch television. Darlene didn't understand why Amity brought him, but she supposed he was companionship. And she envied her cousin even the dull company Axelson must be.

Charlie Hughes told his sister Fiona that most guys play around a little, it doesn't mean anything, don't be so hard on Will.

"How many of them are arrested for murder?"

Charlie shrugged. "You've got a point. How did he land Andrew Broom as his lawyer?"

"Is he any good?"

"Where've you been?"

Fiona wondered. Lately it seemed that all kinds of things had been going on around her that she'd had no idea of. Maybe she could handle the thought that Will had got excited by some college girl who worked part-time at the cemetery, a summer thing, whatever. She didn't mean it wasn't serious, but on a scale of 1 to 10, she wouldn't make it a federal case. Regina came by while Charlie was still there.

"Charlie's been telling me most men cat around a little."

"What are you up to, Charlie?" Gina asked suggestively.

"How can I cat around? I'm not even married."

"I see your point."

Fiona sighed. "It was all over last summer. Will told me and I know he's telling the truth."

"Maybe he's got someone else," Charlie said.

"Hey," Regina said, "get out of here. You're a lot of help."

"If the shoe fits . . ."

Charlie was at the door and Gina slipped off a loafer and sailed it at him. She would have hit him if he hadn't ducked outside.

"What's he talking about?"

"Fiona, I doubt that he knows himself. How are you doing?"

"Will's folks took the kids. I'm just sitting here."

"Let's go out, have a bite, then a few drinks."

Fiona felt suddenly tired. The thought of dressing and driving to a restaurant did not appeal. But Gina insisted.

"You can't brood about something like this."

"Let's visit Will too."

"I'll take you there."

They went to the jail first and they let Fiona in but not Gina.

"Is this for conjugal rights?" the uniformed woman asked huskily.

"What?"

"Do you want a room?"

"That would be nice."

It might have been a room in an economy motel except for the mesh over the windows. Will was brought to her and stood inside the closed door. He looked at the bed; he looked at Fiona.

"What's this?"

"She asked if we wanted a room."

"She thinks we want to screw."

Fiona laughed. It had never dawned on her. Will laughed too, and lifted her to her feet and hugged her. They ended up in bed. Who would have thought? It seemed ages since they had done that. It seemed to cheer Will up and that was nice.

"I thought they were going to lock you up," Gina said when Fiona reappeared.

"They gave us a room."

"A room!"

"Conjugal rights," Fiona said, looking away.

Gina was silent on the way to the restaurant, almost sullen, nor did she cheer up when Fiona told her Will had said to say hello. After they had Salisbury steaks and beer Gina became her usual self. Going on to the Hub Cap seemed the obvious next step. There was line dancing and they both got into it and it was the most fun Fiona had had in years.

Charlie told himself he would go back when he was sure Regina wasn't around so he could make sure that Fiona knew what he was saying. Will had picked up with Gina before Helga went back to school the year before, and they had been going at it ever since. Was Fiona really so damned dumb that she didn't know what her own husband was doing? Charlie had expected her to blow up at the suggestion that all men cheated on their wives and all she had done was nod as if this was something she should have known all along.

Working out every day at Lou's Gym and drinking buttermilk and beer and slurping malts and everything that was supposed to add weight had not helped Charlie a bit. He was the same weight he had been in high school, when he'd tried to make the team that Will Foley had starred on. He had never done better than sub on the second team and had seen no action. He would have been happy to get out there and play on the preparation team and let the varsity pound him black and blue but he had been kept on the bench during intersquad practice sessions too. He had never traveled with the team.

Oh, he went to all the games, taking Fiona and her friends along, a goddam chauffeur, ignored by the girls and why not; he would have despised any girl who preferred him to a guy who could make the team. If he'd had any gymnastic ability, he would have tried out for cheerleader, but he knew without trying that he could never make the grade. The very thought of doing a flip from a standing position—forward, let alone backward—brought out a cold sweat. He would break his neck, literally, he was sure of it.

When Will Foley came to Charlie and said he would like to meet Fiona, Charlie would have handed her over drugged and bound. He couldn't believe it.

"Remember who he is," he had urged Fiona.

"Will Foley."

"Will Foley, athlete. Will Foley, halfback. Will Foley, man of the year."

"You sound like you want to go out with him yourself."

He slapped her, hard, and then spent half an hour making sure he hadn't left a mark on her. He tried to tell her what to wear; he wanted to tell her to put out if Will wanted it, this was her chance. But for once he thought maybe she knew things he didn't. In no time she had Will Foley eating out of her hand. He hadn't laid a glove on her after three dates and he asked her to the Homecoming Dance.

"What do you think of him, Fiona?"

She shrugged. "He's all right if you like football."

Of course, Will Foley would talk football, what did she expect? It almost made his breath stop to hear her talk that way about him, as if she were doing him a favor going out with him or something. Her way worked, though, no doubt about it. When Will broke his leg, Fiona visited him every day. Something was going on between them then, Charlie was sure of it, but the one time he tried to find out, Fiona slapped him, hard.

"Why don't you just get a girl and find out for yourself and stop nosing around me."

"If it weren't for me you would never have met Will Foley."

"Will Foley doesn't know you exist."

Maybe not, but everyone knew Will was going with his sister. Charlie made certain of that. But something happened after Will broke his leg and wasn't playing football anymore. Guys were forgetting who he was. Charlie couldn't believe it.

"How's the leg, Will?" Charlie would ask and Will would look at him as if he had to remember who the hell he was.

"It tells me when it's going to rain."

"Hurt?"

It became clear that Will would not be in shape to play again in senior year. So what? He would get it all back in college. Will laughed when Charlie said so.

"First I'd have to get in."

"What do you mean?"

"My grade point average, Charlie. Forget it."

"You can take the SATs over, Will. After all, you were injured, You're a special case. I'll tutor you."

It was Charlie's shame that he was good in class. Half the time he was pretending he didn't know things so he wouldn't stand out from the other guys.

"You mean that?"

"Of course I mean that."

That's when Charlie discovered that Will Foley not only thought he was dumb, he accepted it. He expected not to understand things. There was no drive.

"Will, you've got to play college ball."

"Let me tell you something, Charlie. This is the first time in years when I don't have to be busting my butt at practice or getting knocked around on the field and on some diet to get me ready for the next season."

That should have liberated Charlie from his thraldom to Will. The guy would never dazzle a crowd on the football field again. Given his mental capacity, it was hard to know what kind of work he would do. Whatever, he would simply sink out of sight into the mass of men and do so happily. But Charlie continued to idolize Will. Now he expected a grounded Will Foley to treat him like an equal and he sought Will's advice about gaining weight.

"Most people are trying to take it off, Charlie."

"No matter what I do I can't gain a pound."

"What's your secret?"

Will wasn't putting on weight but he didn't exercise much anymore. After graduation, he got a job on maintenance at Overlook Cemetery, and he was still working there when he and Fiona went off one night and got married by a Justice of the Peace in Michigan. Neither the bride nor the groom could have been happier than Charlie. He felt like stopping strangers on the street and telling them his sister was married to Will Foley.

Within months he heard guys talking about Will's fooling

around. He said nothing, accepting the assumption that this is what married guys did, even guys married as recently as Will Foley. The next day he stopped to see Fiona and she told him she was expecting a baby. It seemed an odd way for Will to celebrate, taking out some other girl.

Charlie began to see it as a merit in Will that he went with so many different women. He couldn't be serious if he always kept moving on to another one. And he always went back to Fiona, never even spending a night away so far as Charlie could tell. Why worry about a quickie now and again if it didn't really change Will's schedule? Every morning he went to work at Overlook; every night he slept in his own house with his wife and now two kids.

But Helga had been different. Helga had become an obsession with Charlie. It was Gladys who told Charlie about it, and he hadn't liked that. Another guy telling him would have been one thing, but a woman and a friend of Fiona's was another.

"I wouldn't spread it around, Gladys."

"If you mean will I tell Fiona, don't be silly."

"These things come and go."

"I hope you're right."

Charlie had kept an eye on the situation all last summer. He was sure that this time Will would bust up his home if the girl was willing. He acted like a teenager around her, really making an ass out of himself. Oh, she was beautiful. Charlie felt something inside himself turn over slowly the first time he talked to Helga and she looked him in the eye. For a moment at least he had claimed her full attention and it seemed to increase his value. If he himself went after Helga, at least he would have been eligible. He had no wife or kids. He wouldn't be cheating on anyone. But how the hell could he compete with Will Foley?

Even so, that is how he began to think of it, as if Will were making out with a girl meant for Charlie while Fiona and the kids thought he was being a good husband and father. For the first time in his life, Charlie began to dislike Will Foley and then to despise him. What the hell was he anyway except a guy who had had a couple of good seasons of high school football and now worked in maintenance at Overlook Cemetery? That was all he was good for. Charlie had gone to Purdue and taken a degree in accounting and came back to Wyler to work on other people's books. It was routine and he liked that, and he was good at what he did. Looked at objectively, and not as a failure to be Will Foley, he had a pretty good life. But he wasn't getting any younger and he no longer felt like boasting that his sister was married to Will Foley.

Before Helga went back to Bloomington, Will was running around with Regina; so much for the thought that Helga was different. Charlie went to talk to Helga.

"I am Fiona Foley's brother." She had pulled her tractor mower into the shade and was drinking from a water bottle.

"So?"

"She's Will Foley's wife."

She considered that. "What do you want?"

"Not only is he cheating on his wife, he's cheating on you."

"How can he cheat on me?" It pained her to ask the question. She obviously did not want to be involved in this conversation.

"He's seeing another girl too."

"Too?"

"I know about you and Will."

"Have you talked to him about it?"

"I thought I should talk to you."

She leaned toward him and her T-shirt clung to her body. "Will told me about you, you creep. Just stay away from me, do you understand? I don't care about your silly gossip. If you come near me again I'll tell Will and I don't know what he'll do to you."

"Do you think he cares about you?"

He wanted to tell her that she should not waste herself on a guy like that; he wanted her to look at him and suddenly see that Charlie Hughes was the sort of man she really wanted. But she glared at him with contemptuous anger. Then she pulled the choke and the motor of the tractor roared in protest. She put it in gear and he had to dance out of the way as she started off. He stared after her. A minute before he had loved her, but love had turned to hatred.

Andrew had sent flowers to Mrs. Bjornsen, courtesy of the firm whose summer intern her daughter had been, he had left a message on her phone and on the third day, wondering what funeral arrangements had been made, he suggested to Gerald that they stop by the Bjornsen home. But the visit had seemed less imperative than the round of golf Gerald had suggested.

"I mean it as a business conference."

Gerald was not being facetious. Uncle and nephew had their best exchanges while golfing, each playing well enough to enjoy the exercise and free his mind for the kind of easy exchange that was not always possible in the office.

"What's the agenda?"

"This will sound crazy. The will we finally got a glimpse of, Stanley Waggoner's original?"

"For God's sake don't let that get out. Frank McGough would have a legitimate complaint for a change and he would go after Judge Glacer relentlessly."

"To say nothing of you."

"To say nothing of me."

What had caught Gerald's attention was the group of heirs apparent that Jeb Riverside had banded together. Eight were listed and Gerald was doing a routine check on the claimants, not with the intent to weasel out of the last will and testament of Stanley Waggoner but because Catherine had shown some curiosity about these people whose blood Stanley had acknowledged to be at least fractionally the same as his.

"Two are dead, Andrew. One in an accident, the other the victim of a break-in at her home."

Andrew had taken out a cigar. He rolled it in his fingers and waited.

"I called a man who lives just west of Chicago, Jonathan Apple, and found that he is just recovering from a near-fatal accident. The woman I talked to said he was lucky to be alive."

"Hmmm."

"The next name on the list is Darlene B. Larson."

"Darlene. That's the name of Helga's mother."

"This isn't her. Not unless she was born twenty-two years ago."

"Are the birth dates in the will?"

"I had Susannah do some checking and she got this match from the courthouse."

"That's the kind of work someone like Helga should be doing."

"Andrew, I think this is Helga."

"Why?"

Gerald had said this was far-fetched and it did indeed seem a tangent to the work that was occupying them—until he came to Helga, that is. "How do you get from Darlene H. Larson to Helga Bjornsen?"

"On the birth certificate the mother is given as Darlene Larson."

"Who's she?"

"Mrs. Bjornsen."

"How so?"

"She married him two years later. Mark Larson. It lasted less than a year.

He went back to Norway she went back to her maiden name."

"So now we have Darlene Bjornsen."

"And her daughter Darlene Helga Bjornsen."

That is when they did a U-turn just short of the entrance to the club and headed back to town and to the little frame house under the huge shade trees. Andrew was turning over in his mind what Gerald was suggesting. The list of acknowledged claimants to some portion of Stanley Waggoner's money was seemingly being winnowed. Gerald had turned up several violent and unexpected deaths. But caution was required. From the Kennedy assassination to the Foster suicide, it was possible to amass lists of mysterious and unexplained deaths. On the basis of such lists complicated conspiracy theories were raised. If that is all there had been, Andrew would not have suggested the serious step of postponing their golf game. It was the apparent inclusion of Helga on the list that convinced him Gerald was on to something.

"Good work, Gerald."

"If this is true, we have one big job, not two small ones."

"There are not many who would refer to the disposition of the Waggoner money as a small problem."

"Or the death of a young woman not yet out of college."

Gerald drove into the driveway, which was hardly more than dirt that was more beaten down than what would have been the lawn, and came to a stop. Andrew was knocking on the door before Gerald got out of the car. Mrs. Bjornsen was apparently a recluse, only the reporter Rebecca Prell seemed to have induced her to talk at any length, but Andrew intended to overpower her with the urgency of the questions Gerald's inquiries led to.

What was her connection to the Waggoner family?

How had her daughter's name ended up on a list of claimants that Stanley Waggoner had approved?

He rapped on the door more insistently and turned to Gerald, who was now beside him.

"Who was listed as father on that birth certificate?"

"A most prolific fellow."

"Who?"

"John Doe."

Andrew now banged on the door with the heel of his hand. From the near distance a siren was audible. As they stood there, the siren grew closer, distracting them from their impatience as they waited for the door to open. And then the sheriff's car appeared and came tearing down the street toward them. To their astonishment it turned in at the driveway and came to a halt behind their car, the two doors opening as it did and a deputy appearing on each side of the car. Behind them the door of the house was pulled open and a figure in a kimono pushed past them, running toward the deputies. She turned, her face a mask of terror, pointing at Andrew and Gerald.

"Take them away! Make them stop lurking about this house!"

"Mrs. Bjornsen," Andrew said, starting toward her.

A piercing scream split the air and Mrs. Bjornsen cowered in fear against the uniformed chest of a deputy.

Sheriff Cleary drove out to the scene of the complaint with pardonable anticipation. He had the message repeated, lest there be any mistake.

"Andrew Broom and Gerald Rowan have been harassing a widow, trespassing on her property and scaring her half to death?"

"Sheriff, I am reading it just as I wrote it down. I read it back to her and she said, yes, that is exactly what she is charging."

"Hold everything until I get there."

"We can handle this," Phelps said gruffly.

"Of course you can. But can you enjoy it as much as I will?"

On any other day of the week. Sheriff Cleary would have been the first to praise Andrew Broom. His voice would be loud in the chorus of those who saw Andrew as an unequivocal asset to Wyler, Indiana, its present and future. That one should also resent such a paragon of civic virtue was a truth less universally acknowledged. But it was a species of resentment Sheriff Cleary felt, and exhilaration, now that he was on his sirened way to mediate between Andrew and a poor widow woman who insisted on swearing out a formal complaint against him.

Andrew was the picture of repose when Cleary drove in and they both waited for his siren to die away completely. Phelps came forward but a disheveled woman in a kimono, her hair wild on her head, rushed up to Cleary.

"Are you the sheriff?"

"Yes, ma'am."

"Arrest those two!"

"In a minute, in a minute. Just what exactly is going on?"

They all circled the woman as she talked, her voice riding up and down the scale. For two days, she had been aware of people creeping around outside her windows; she had actually spent hours in a cedar closet that locked from within, certain that they had come for her.

"Who would that be?"

"The same ones who murdered Helga!"

With the mention of her daughter's name, the hysterical frenzy that had sustained her gave way to inconsolable sobbing. Cleary wasn't finding the scene a bit enjoyable.

"And these are the men who have been frightening you?"

She scarcely looked at Andrew and Gerald. "I never saw them. They were always in the dark, or shadows, out of sight, but I could hear them."

Cleary exchanged a glance with Phelps. The deputy was beginning to wonder at the wisdom of putting himself and the department at the disposal of a woman whose grip on reality seemed weak. Cleary took the woman's arm and led her slowly toward the house. On the porch they sat side by side on the swing. Cleary spoke soothingly to the woman, who from time to time shuddered. She lay her head briefly on his shoulder and then sat upright. Calm was returning.

He assured her that he would leave a deputy on duty there for at least the next twenty-four hours.

"But those are the men," she whispered.

"I don't think so. Do you recognize them?"

"No."

"I do. I don't think they have been creeping around your property. But I will question them and make certain. Meanwhile I will post a deputy here."

Phelps did not like the idea of being left carless with a woman whose hysteria had been hair-raising only minutes before.

"I'll take Schneider with me. We'll leave the car." Cleary added, "For easier communication."

Cleary decided to ride with the two lawyers. Gerald backed slowly out of the driveway after the sheriff's vehicles had cleared the way.

"Now, what the hell was that all about, Andrew?"

"You heard the woman. Someone has been creeping around her house in the dark, scaring her to death."

"She thinks it was you."

"Well, it was someone."

"You sure? Up close, there was a definite smell of alcohol on her breath."

"You mean we are not under arrest?"

"Not this time, Andrew."

At Andrew's office Cleary sat while the two lawyers laid out a scenario that sounded nuttier than anything Mrs. Bjornsen could come up with.

"Her daughter worked here?"

"As an intern. Just a couple of weeks, but long enough for Gerald to fall in love with her."

"That was a matter of minutes," Gerald said.

Insofar as Cleary understood it, and Andrew swore he'd have his badge if he breathed a word of this before its time, there was the possibility that someone was knocking off the little group Stanley Waggoner had acknowledged as blood heirs, however remote. Gerald put a copy of the list in front of Cleary, with lines drawn through some names, followed by a date.

"That's when they were removed from the list by the Grim Reaper."

According to Gerald, Darlene H. Nelson was Helga, the girl whose dead body had been found a few days before in a car parked in Overlook Cemetery.

"Let me stop you right there, Gerald. You know full well we've already got a man under arrest for that, your client Will Foley. He was fooling around with the girl last summer but now he's got a new girl and last summer's was an impediment."

"So he killed her?"

"I won't bore you with all the evidence that points to him."

"Go ahead. As you say, Foley is my client."

It seemed a good chance to let Andrew know what they were up against defending Foley. The trouble with evidence is that, when you lay it out you expect a skeptical reaction and that is what Cleary got from both Andrew and Gerald. That the body had been found in Foley's vehicle, and that only then did the guy claim it was stolen, drew only a downturned mouth and a nod.

"Don't you recognize a frame-up, Maurice?"

"Is that going to be your defense?"

"I doubt this will ever come to trial."

"I'd rather have my story than yours, Andrew."

"Well, I'm glad you sensed the importance of providing protection for that poor woman."

Phelps? How could they have gotten out of there without leaving a deputy? But Cleary was not loath to take praise when it came.

"We'll protect her against real or imaginary prowlers."

"Oh, they're real enough," Andrew said.

Gerald had wondered why Andrew was so generous, telling Cleary about what had suddenly suggested itself. But it all came down to that final remark. Andrew wanted Cleary to take seriously the danger Mrs. Bjornsen was facing.

"Whatever Helga would have inherited should go to her mother. If Helga was a victim of someone winnowing the list, her mother is now as vulnerable as the daughter was."

"I said it sounds far-fetched, and it does. Cleary's reaction is what we can expect."

"That's because it's only a theory. We have to tie it down to evidence."

"What would you suggest?"

"Right now? Hitting a bucket of balls."

Andrew wasn't suggesting a drive out to the country club

practice range but to Lefty's Hook, a seedy range west of town that had more kids in the batting cages than golfers slamming balls out onto the unwatered range. The distance signs were faded numerals painted on boards that leaned this way and that. They looked as if a direct hit would flatten them. Apparently, Andrew thought they could think better there, though it was difficult to say on what basis. He had been silent on the drive, after giving directions. Andrew didn't open the passenger door when Gerald parked.

"Ever been here before?"

"Nope."

"The man who runs it is Jeb Riverside."

Then Andrew got it. Riverside was not only on the list, he had been the one responsible for the pooling of interests so that they could present Stanley Waggoner with something like a class action claim. But Stanley had wanted only proof of their status and then had acquiesced without a fight. If some of the same blood flowed in his veins and in theirs, he would be happy to share the family wealth and provide for them in his will. The subsequent arrangement with Catherine had not changed that.

"Is he here?"

Andrew nodded toward the range, where a tractor protected by mesh armor was going back and forth, picking up balls. The driver wore what looked like an NFL helmet. A good idea. A couple of teenagers seemed to think that the point of hitting balls was to nail the guy on the tractor. They were trying so hard that Riverside was safe. Gerald found himself imagining how he could take a five iron and whistle a ball at the tractor.

"Where are your binoculars?"

165

This was a kind of joke. Andrew had come into Gerald's office a few weeks before to find him at the window looking across at the windows of another building. Andrew stood beside his nephew and silently followed the animated conversation between two girls. They held cups of coffee, presumably they were on break, and they made a lovely picture. That afternoon, Andrew had dropped a pair of binoculars on Gerald's desk.

"To facilitate your bird-watching."

Gerald had taken them down to his car and put them in the glove compartment. Now he took them from Andrew and brought them to his eyes. He searched for and found the tractor and then he had the driver's face. He followed him back and forth until he was sure he would recognize him anywhere.

"What's under the helmet?"

"Hair. Lots of it."

"We going to hit a bucket of balls?"

"Let's go pick up Susannah and have dinner at the club."

Clearly, Andrew wanted Susannah brought up to speed on the list of claimants. She had checked out the birth certificate for Gerald but he had still been too excited and unsure of his epiphany to tell her. First he wanted Andrew to hear it. If his uncle dismissed it, all right.

But Andrew had embraced it more enthusiastically than Gerald himself. Now he felt an obligation to urge the defects in the idea.

"Cleary is right, Andrew. There may be holes in the case against Will Foley, but it is a case."

Susannah became Gerald's ally. Whatever else could be said about the names that had been stricken from the list, their bearers had lived far from Wyler. If there was something going on, it did not fall to Andrew to pursue it. His task was to protect the interests of Catherine. She had slipped away for a visit home as well as to the nursing home where her life had taken such a dramatic turn. Andrew frowned again, as he had at the house when Susannah told him this.

"I wish she were here with us now."

"Good heavens, you don't think she is in any danger, do you?"

Andrew was tempted to answer but did not. "Gerald, are you free to drive to Schaumburg, Illinois, tomorrow?"

"Sonny Apple?"

Later that night Gerald called Julie at her private number and asked if she would let him drive her across a state line tomorrow.

"What state line?"

"Illinois."

"Chicago?" There was a lilt in her voice.

"And beyond."

"I don't know."

She wanted to be persuaded, and Gerald was happy to oblige. If there had been any insuperable obstacle, Julie would have mentioned it immediately. The price of her company on the morrow was a stop in Chicago.

"Where?"

"The Marriott?"

His pulse raced. "An overnighter?"

"In separate rooms, needless to say. At your expense."

"It's a deal."

"Will you get that gurgle out of your voice? This is not our honeymoon."

"Just a dress rehearsal?"

167

"Dress has nothing to do with it."

The phone went dead. What a tease. Gerald was no more interested than Julie, not really, in anticipating the joys of marriage. He wanted their union public and aboveboard and universally celebrated, and there were many obstacles to overcome before that could be. Meanwhile, they must settle for such junkets as the one they would take on the morrow.

The Schaumberg police had questioned Sonny Apple about
his friends and enemies when his accident was ruled not to
have been an accident but a deliberate attempt to disable his
car.

"You anger some patron of the library or anything like that?"
Bingham was the male member of the interrogation team that
had come to his bedside. He asked questions as if he wondered
what Farthing, his partner, would think. Not much, it appeared, when Bingham explored the possibility that Sonny had
wittingly or unwittingly excited a patron of the Schaumberg
library to murderous impulses.

"How much do you have to do with patrons?" Farthing
asked. She was the same height as Bingham and had round eyes

with white all around the brown irises. This gave her the look of an owl.

"I run a specialized program. How to create your genealogy."

"Get along well with people?" Bingham asked.

Cynthia stirred in her chair. "They all love him." Sonny half hoped and half feared that she would come to his bed and hug him, as if to underscore what she said.

"That's not much of a parking lot, is it?"

"Parking lot?" Farthing looked at her partner as if she would like to tear off his epaulets.

"People quarrel over parking spaces. Remember the Dishwell case."

Sonny remembered it. A woman named Dishwell zipped into a just-vacated parking space that another motorist had been waiting to occupy. When he remonstrated, she gave him the finger and went about her business. When she returned to her car and got behind the wheel, a man stepped up to the window and emptied his revolver into her. He was never identified.

"We have designated parking spaces. The staff."

The interview went on like that and did little to alleviate the unnerving realization that someone had fixed his car so it would spin out of control, presumably when he was in heavy traffic, with presumably grisly results. Well, he had survived, but somewhere the person who did it might be planning another try. Cynthia said she would never leave his side. He was flat on his back when he married her. Sonny looked forward to getting out of his body cast. Meanwhile, Cynthia was attentive and perhaps just slightly suffocating in her devotion.

It was thanks to Cynthia that he had a constant and orderly stream of visitors from the library. But she was visibly pleased when Gerald Rowan and Julie McGough showed up to see Sonny.

"Do you know Sonny?" she asked when she let them in.

"I know of him," Gerald said affably, his tone suggesting his sense of good fortune in having even so tenuous a connection with Cynthia's husband. "This is Julie McGough, my legal assistant."

"You're a lawyer?" Wariness crept unbidden into Cynthia's voice.

"I represent a relative of Jonathan Apple's."

"Everyone calls him Sonny."

"I didn't want to presume."

"What is the relative's name?"

"Stanley Waggoner."

Her brow clouded. "Isn't that a coincidence."

"What do you mean?"

"Sonny had a visitor two days ago about the same relative. From a sort of relative of his."

"I wonder who that would be."

"Jeb Riverside."

Sonny, when Cynthia had introduced the guests and gotten everyone settled around his bed, was glad to explain how Jeb Riverside had first gotten in touch with him via E-mail.

"I had put my genealogical data on my personal page on the web. This caught his attention. And earned his displeasure."

"How so?" Julie asked.

"He thought it would attract more claimants to the Waggoner fortune. I had no idea there was any such fortune or that it concerned me. Then I saw the link that Riverside had noticed but which had not previously struck me. Some elementary research showed me that I was indeed related, though

171

remotely, to the family that had produced the legendary Waggoner automobile. Even so, it was like hearing that you were related to the founder of Wells-Fargo. Riverside convinced me otherwise."

"Your wife tells me he has visited you recently."

"Checking up on a fellow heir." Sonny laughed. Cynthia did not join in.

"You have seen the list of the other claimants, I am sure."

"Oh yes."

"Did Riverside mention that a number have dropped off the list?"

"Didn't he say someone died, Cynthia?"

Cynthia sensed that Gerald Rowan had arrived quickly at the purpose of his visit. He pulled his chair up next to Sonny and spread a copy of the list on the cover of the manila folder he had taken it from. He ticked off the deaths that had considerably reduced the list.

"Mr. Apple, your supposed accident was meant to remove you from the list."

Cynthia let out a cry. "I knew it, I knew it. I thought there was some connection the moment Riverside arrived."

"Connection," Sonny said, laughing. "What kind of connection?"

She looked at Gerald Rowan. He said, "I am not prepared to be that specific, but you may very well be right. In any case, someone who would gain from the winnowing of the list seems to have put his mind to lessening the number of slices in the pie."

"But each heir would gain from there being a smaller number."

"Each surviving heir," said Gerald Rowan.

Gerald and Julie dined in Old Town and had a couple of drinks before returning to the Marriott about midnight. There was a message from Andrew saying he had received the message Gerald had left and to call him no matter what time it was.

"Why are you spending the night in Chicago?" Andrew asked when Gerald got through to him. "You could have been home by now."

Julie had come to his room preparatory to going down to the bar off the lobby. His excuse was that there might be a message from Andrew and he would not leave her just hanging around the lobby waiting.

"I am perfectly safe," she scoffed.

"I was thinking of the cream of Chicago youth."

"It seemed a good chance to get together with a friend," he said to Andrew.

A pause. "Anyone I know?"

"She's someone I very much want you to know and like."

Andrew's tone brightened. "I'm looking forward to it. Don't hurry back. I've put Broadbeck on the detail."

"Good."

"How is Jonathan Apple doing?"

"He's on the mend. He has married since the attempt on his life and has a very devoted and protective wife. I doubt that anyone will get near enough to harm him again. Riverside was already here."

"I wish we had thought of Broadbeck earlier, Gerald."

"We lacked a few premises. Mrs. Apple was wary of Riverside."

"As well she might be."

"I'll see you tomorrow."

"No need to hurry. Do you have your phone with you?"

"In the car."

"I'll call if there is reason to. But just relax and have a good time. Look, bring her back with you if she's agreeable."

It was unfair to make Andrew think that by lingering in Chicago he was weakening in his attachment to Julie Mc-Gough. But of course Andrew had jumped at the conclusion he wanted to reach. Gerald hoped he wasn't doing the same in the case of Jeb Riverside.

Downstairs they nursed a drink and talked, Gerald musing that he might very well have begun his legal career in this city rather than succumbing to his Uncle Andrew's case for joining him in Wyler, Indiana.

"I have to tell you that most of my friends and law school professors thought I was making the wrong choice."

"Maybe they were right."

"One plus I would not have known then: if I weren't working with Andrew there would be no impediment to our going together."

"But if you hadn't come to Wyler you would never have met me."

"That was another plus I didn't know of at the time."

"Plus in which direction?"

"Pluses always read to the right."

"No, they are symmetrical. Two plus three and three plus two come to the same thing."

"I was thinking of one plus one."

She sighed. "Isn't it silly that two grown-ups should permit a father and an uncle to dictate to them what they may do?"

"What's the solution?"

"I could have my church wedding. I could have the whole thing, but if my father didn't attend I would be devastated."

"He couldn't keep away."

"You must know him well enough by now to see that he would."

"So would Andrew."

"So what is the solution?"

Despite their seeming despair of any solution, they both were certain that eventually there would be one. And not just eventually, soon.

"We could elope, have a civil ceremony and then return and you could demand the big wedding."

"And between the two ceremonies?"

"I would be a monk."

"You might come to like it."

"You could tempt me."

"I wouldn't know how." She reached across the table and moved her finger gently over his lips. He did the same for her.

"This would do very nicely."

Andrew had called old Broadbeck up to his office from his lair in the basement of the building and outlined the project for him. "Your son Emil still in town?"

Broadbeck looked insulted at this apparent lapse of memory. "He runs the golf shop at Hiawatha."

"The public course."

"He gives a few lessons."

Emil had placed second in the state tournament a decade before, and in Andrew's estimation, it had ruined the boy's life. Emil was a good golfer, but he had played over his head to come in second. He had never done so well again, but he had been bitten by the bug. He was certain he was meant to be a professional golfer. He had tried to qualify for the Open

year after year without success. He had applied for admission
to the PGA school for aspiring professional golfers and been
refused. But these reversals strengthened rather than weakened
his conviction that he was meant to rise to the first ranks of
celebrity golfers. Meanwhile, he subsisted on odd golf-related
jobs in the area. Andrew knew of Emil's fill-in job at Hiawatha
but wanted to give Broadbeck Senior the satisfaction of telling
him.

"Didn't he work for Jeb Riverside for a while?"

Old Broadbeck's normally pleasant expression was replaced
with one of anger. "That son of a bitch."

"What happened there anyway?"

Not remarkably articulate at the best of times, old Broadbeck told the story in broken phrases and bursts of profanity.
It had been Emil's understanding that Riverside would sponsor
him in his bid for a spot in the U.S. Open. All Emil had to
do was a few odd jobs around Lefty's Hook while he spent
the day in practice. Riverside would pay for transportation,
lodging and meals as Emil moved up the levels of competition
and clinched a spot in the open field. As it turned out, Riverside had reneged. Free buckets of balls and the use of the
range in return for a few hours behind the counter and a
pickup with the tractor several times a day. But transportation
and board and room? Emil had to be kidding.

"How did Emil do that year?"

He had been eliminated in Wyler, not even getting to Indianapolis. For anyone else this would have made the misun-
derstanding between Emil and Riverside moot, but for Emil
and his father it was the principle of the thing. It was only a
fluke that Emil had been eliminated, some damned dentist
from Muncie sandbagging him on the back nine. The fact that

Riverside had been unable to enact his treachery did not make him less of a skunk to the Broadbecks.

"Tell Emil that I will sponsor him this year."

"You mean that?"

"I'll back him as far as he can go. I'll get him a visitor's pass at the country club valid up to the date of the first qualifying round."

Old Broadbeck was overwhelmed. Would Andrew tell Emil this news himself?

"Coming from you direct it will mean much more."

"Have him come see me."

Emil was at the office next morning when Susannah arrived to open up. She put him in a chair from which he could look out over the city and its environs from Andrew's twelfth-floor aerie in the Hoosier Towers.

"My father said he wanted to see me."

"Oh, he's expecting you."

Andrew overheard this exchange when he came in and he called out, "Susannah, is Emil Broadbeck here yet?"

Emil levitated from the chair he sat in and came toward Andrew as if he had just placed his drive precisely where he had wanted and couldn't wait to take a second shot that would put his ball on the green, in position for an eagle.

Andrew repeated to Emil the offer he had made to the young man's father the night before.

"I can't tell you what your confidence in me means, Mr. Broom."

"Do the best you can, that's all I ask."

"Mr. Broom, is there anything I can do for you?"

"Well, I wouldn't want to ask you to do anything that would take your mind off your goal."

Emil laughed. "Nothing could do that."

Andrew leaned forward and Emil drew his chair closer to the desk. In a lowered voice, Andrew said, "I think you and I have the same opinion of Jeb Riverside."

"That son of a bitch." Immediately, Emil clamped a hand over his mouth and looked over his shoulder at the door, fearful that Susannah might have heard.

"From what your father told me, you have a right to a little profanity. The thing you could do for me, but only if you promise it won't interfere with your preparation for the Open, concerns Jeb Riverside."

"I'll do it. Whatever it is, I'll do it."

"I want a 'round-the-clock watch on Jeb Riverside. Maybe for several weeks. I want to know where he is and what he is doing all the time."

Andrew might have said more, telling Emil what it was that prompted this curiosity about Jeb Riverside, but Emil needed no further incentive to do what he was being asked to do. His father could spell him for five or six hours during the day and Emil would do the rest.

"When do I start?"

"As soon as we make arrangements for you to practice at the country club. After this little surveillance job, you'll want to buckle down."

Emil left with the assurance that he was beginning immediately after he told his dad what the two of them were going to be doing.

When the door closed behind Emil, Andrew hoped he had provided at least some insurance against a recurrence of what had happened to Helga and what had nearly happened to Sonny Apple. If he was right, and Riverside was behind these mysterious deaths and accidents, surveillance of his actions would protect everyone on the list. But he felt glad that there was extra protection for Mrs. Bjornsen in the person of Cleary's deputy.

"You want to deputize a few men for that task, Maurice, I'll donate their salaries."

"Andrew," Cleary replied, "I am not doing this as a favor to you. This is part of my duty as sheriff. I do have some good news for you though."

"What's that?"

"I convinced Mrs. Bjornsen not to bring charges of trespass against you and Gerald."

Andrew suggested that the sheriff engage in a gymnastic act clearly beyond the present capacities of Maurice Cleary.

34

His code name on the web was Schmuck, not a very imaginative choice, but all the good names he thought up were already taken, so he settled for Schmuck, rightly guessing that no one would willingly call himself that. It had been a load he had carried since he was a kid, that name. Once he asked his father why they didn't change it, but Schmucker Senior had not understood the desire. He looked at Junius in genuine puzzlement. Your name was who you were; change your name and you would cease to exist. That prospect, anything having to do with the reality of death, put Schmucker Senior off, an odd attitude for the owner of two cemeteries. But then he had spent almost no time in the sexton's office, preferring to swelter in the greenhouse attached to his garage where he cultivated plants exotic for the region. The only place they could survive was in the greenhouse, which was electrically heated nine months out of the year. Junius's image of his father was of a moon-faced moist-eyed man peering through foliage.

The greenhouse had been his father's escape from reality, Junius saw that later when he replicated his father's reclusive impulse by shutting himself up in the sexton's office. He had married Gloria because she was the girl his mother had chosen for him. Maybe he wouldn't have found anyone otherwise. Gloria now weighed well over two hundred pounds and their daughter favored her mother, if that was the phrase. Junius himself was large, but he felt larger next to his wife. Somewhere over the past ten years they had struck an unspoken bargain more or less to lead their own lives. Sleeping with Gloria had never been a treat, but that had stopped by mutual consent and Gloria had her own room now. Junius might have had two daughters, is what it came down to. His interest in computers proved to be distraction enough from the lingering desires of the flesh, but gradually the distraction and the desires had merged when the web became accessible and presented an explosion of home pages, services, you name it. The first time Junius happened upon a pornographic site he had been shocked and had immediately hit the Back button and cleared the screen. But the image lingered, and he took another look.

There are moments in a man's life that divide the past decisively from the present, and that had been such a moment in Junius's life. At first he kidded himself that he was just surfing to see how bad things were but within a week the computer had become little more than an instrument of long-distance titillation for him. He kept the blinds between his office and Gladys's closed, not that he imagined she had any idea what he was doing in there. The fact was that 90 percent of the population, maybe more, had no idea that a computer could put at your fingertips what men had previously gone in furtive and expensive pursuit of. All Junius had to do was settle into his chair, hit a couple of keys, and he had before his eyes what King Farouk had spent a fortune on.

For some time it was just his secret vice, confined to his office at Overlook. When he went home at night, he tried to scrub his mind and imagination clear of the images he had been seeing on the screen of his monitor. He did not have a computer at home. To install one would have been like fouling his nest. Nights, he read western novels or watched television, more often than not in the basement den. The VCR had been an unwise purchase. The one in the family room had expanded the pleasures of Gloria and their daughter, enabling them to substitute rented videos for the scheduled televised fare. Junius installed one in the basement den so he could watch the westerns he alone enjoyed. But soon he was sending off for x-rated videos and watching them at home while above him his bloated wife and daughter watched more edifying fare.

From time to time he tried to break the grip pornography had on him, but he simply did not have the will to do so. After all, what difference did it make? On the several Sundays a year he accompanied his family to church, he found himself wondering what he was doing there, but the preacher's insistence that they were all miserable sinners proved to be a consolation. If what he was doing was sinful, it was only to be expected.

Junius never connected the antics on his monitor or the videos on the VCR with Gloria. His wife and daughter might have belonged to a different species from the wantons who performed for the camera, performing deeds which, though they had first disgusted Junius, came to seem normal. He began to wonder if Gladys was at all like the girls on the screen.

Standing at the pulled blinds, he could lift a blade a millimeter and study her at work. He found it difficult to imagine her doing what the girls on the web did. It was the golden-haired Helga who might have stepped off the screen of the monitor when she came to apply for a job.

Charlie Hughes had told Rebecca Prell what a wonderful guy Will Foley was. When she found out that Fiona Foley was Charlie's sister, Rebecca figured Will Foley's number-one fan didn't know what a rotten husband he was. She might have just written him off as a dum-dum if she hadn't seen him out with Regina Foote. The next day she accepted a date with Emil Broadbeck.

"You don't want to see a movie?" Emil asked, obviously disappointed. He liked being alone in the dark. She didn't mind it herself. It was better than listening to him recount every single stroke in his last golf outing.

"Let's just have a couple of drinks and talk."

"Where?"

She mentioned the country and western bar she had quite

by accident seen Charlie and Regina go into. A wild idea, as if they would be there two nights in a row. She knew Emil liked country and western, so he agreed and they got a little table and the girl brought them beer and on the little stage in back the music went on nonstop. From ten to eleven was amateur hour and people went onstage and sang the way they did in the shower and usually were hooted down before they got too far.

"I never been here before," Emil said, liking what he saw. The girls favored very short dresses and scoop-necked blouses. And boots, which did not do a lot for their legs but were a necessity for the stomping that punctuated the dancing.

"Neither have I."

"How'd you hear of it?"

"I just drove past and it looked good."

The place was filled with smoke. You could quit smoking and go right on smoking here. Rebecca was not a nut about tobacco but this was pretty bad. When Regina and Charlie came in, it took a while before Rebecca was sure it was the two of them. They came through the smoke and were put at a table not far off. Regina looked around as if making the point that she really wasn't with the guy she was with, and Charlie noticed this, Rebecca was sure of it. What a twit.

Rebecca's theory was that, no matter how dumb Charlie seemed to be in the case of Helga, he knew Will had been taking out Regina and he was taking her out so that . . . Well, it was a pretty complicated theory, but she understood what she meant. He was being a Will Foley substitute and that made him important. So why did she go out with him? Probably because at the moment the alternative was staying home.

Emil agreed to dance somewhat reluctantly although why

was a matter for wonderment, he was so graceful on the floor. He caught the eye of Regina, in the sense that she followed him about the floor with a smoldering gaze; Charlie watched her watching the other men with seeming equanimity. Strange fellow, Rebecca thought. Perhaps Will Foley had assigned him the task of squiring his squeeze while he was out of circulation.

What would happen to Foley? The circumstantial case against him was strong, but Foster laughed away the evidence when Rebecca listed it for him.

"It doesn't matter."

"The body of last summer's girlfriend found in a car that he then decides has been stolen doesn't matter?"

"Andrew Broom is defending him."

Foster was to Andrew as Charlie was to Will Foley, apparently, a hero-worshiper. Rebecca had her own reasons to admire Andrew Broom and she would not have objected if Gerald Rowan, his nephew and partner, noticed her existence, but that did not lessen the fact that the evidence against Will Foley was overwhelming.

"If I were on the jury I would vote to convict."

"But you're prejudiced."

"Prejudiced! Is being influenced by the evidence a sign of prejudice?"

"I tell you it doesn't matter."

"You think Andrew Broom can clear a guilty man?"

Foster was shocked. "Certainly not. You've missed my point. If Andrew undertook to defend Will Foley it is because he believes he is an innocent man."

"But he could be wrong."

Foster smiled indulgently. Rebecca let it go. If she had gone on, she would have pointed out that it was Gerald Rowan who was the de facto defender of Will Foley, and Gerald Rowan, the last time she had heard, was neither infallible nor invincible.

"It looks bad," Gerald had admitted the last time she talked to him about the case.

"Bad! He should be grateful there isn't a death penalty in the state."

"There are some extenuating circumstances."

"His car was stolen?"

"If it was, that changes everything, right?"

"If."

That night she had done breathing exercises for half an hour, squeezing from her heart and mind anything remotely resembling prejudice. She tried not to take pleasure from the prospect that this time Andrew Broom would fall on his face and Gerald Rowan with him. She had worn her new yellow dress to the interview with Gerald but she might just as well have worn coveralls.

"How you liking Wyler?" he asked, almost as an afterthought.

"I've been here a year."

"That long?"

"I miss the social life I knew, of course, but this is a great professional opportunity."

"The *Dealer*? I guess you're right. You would be a better judge of such things."

"It doesn't leave me much time for my social life."

"The price of ambition." He sighed.

Was he really that opaque? But she knew the problem was Julie McGough, the breathtakingly beautiful daughter of Andrew Broom's arch rival, Frank McGough. The two had to

meet in out-of-the-way improbable places, lest they be discovered.

"Gerald Rowan just came in," Emil now whispered in her
ear. "Pretend you don't know him."

"Why?"

"I am on assignment starting tomorrow. Very hush-hush."

She stared at Emil. His eyes narrowed significantly and he
pressed her hand.

"It may be weeks before we can have a night like this again."

"What will you be doing?" Gerald and Julie had found a
table the length of the building from the band. They disappeared from sight.

"It's why I wanted to go to a movie," Emil confided.

"What is this special assignment?"

"It's confidential, Rebecca."

"That doesn't mean you can't tell me."

"A reporter!"

"Is that all I am to you, a reporter?" She turned away, she
refused to let him take her hand; only gradually did she allow
herself to be cajoled into listening to his confidence. She turned
and put her hands over his, expressive of her pleasure in his
trust, anxious to hear more.

"Jeb Riverside?"

"The son of a bitch."

"Emil!"

"I use the phrase advisedly. Have I ever told you what he
did to me?"

In detail, several times. This was one source of Rebecca's
surprise that he would accept any task that involved Jeb Riverside. Another source was that Andrew Broom should turn

to Emil. Willy-nilly, this led her to think that the assignment was not that important.

"What are you supposed to watch for?"

"I will watch his movements at all times."

"I understand that. But why?"

"I can't tell you."

"Emil!"

"I don't know myself. They didn't say and I figured if they felt I had to know they would tell me."

"Let's dance."

She maneuvered them across the floor in the direction of the table Gerald and Julie had taken. The two were necking shamelessly. Rebecca angrily steered in the opposite direction. Had she thought she could excite Gerald's curiosity, even his interest in her, by gliding past his table in the arms of another man? It looked as if a fifty-piece band could march unnoticed past that table.

"Who's that good-looking girl with the large earrings?" Emil asked after they had returned to their table.

"So you finally noticed."

"I thought she was looking at somebody behind me."

It was one of Emil's charms, his diffidence about his physical attractions. Perhaps Regina Foote wouldn't even notice that Emil was not destined to move in the fast track intellectually.

"Go ahead and make goo-goo eyes back at her. Don't mind me."

"I said I wanted to go to a movie."

"Let's."

And they did. Emil put his arm around her shoulders and she snuggled up. The movie was half over but they didn't care.

It was one of those times when Rebecca felt she could marry a man she was smarter than and find happiness and contentment. In the darkened theater, his lips hungrily on hers, Emil was the equal of any man.

She took the glow with her to bed and slept with a smile on her lips. In the morning she awoke, floated into the kitchen for juice, turned on the radio, and enjoyed what was left of the wonderful feeling she had known in Emil's arms. The smile faded and she turned toward the radio, as if the better to hear the awful news.

The body of Regina Foote had been found in the backseat of a car earlier that morning.

36

It would of course have been unseemly to celebrate the murder of another young woman, but with their client under lock and key, the twin of the murder he had been arrested for considerably weakened the prosecutor's case. The vehicle in which the body had been found was the same one that had been stolen from Will Foley's garage the first time and in which the body of Helga Bjornsen was discovered. It was Gerald's contention that whoever had done the one did the other and his client could not possibly have done the second. The syllogism impressed Susannah, drew silent but seeming approval from Andrew, but impressed Quarles the prosecutor not a whit.

"A copycat murder," Quarles suggested. "Some nut mimicking Will Foley."

"You're begging the question."

"How so?"

"Will Foley has killed no one."

"We'll let the jury decide that."

"A jury that will know of the killing of Regina Foote."

Quarles waved it away but two hours later he telephoned Gerald and his tone was considerably chastened.

"Did you know about Regina and Foley?"

"Didn't you?"

"No."

No wonder he had been impervious to the logic of Gerald's presentation earlier. Quarles was by no means ready to throw in the towel, but he now saw that the murder of Regina posed large problems for his case against Will Foley.

Item. Regina had died in the same awful way as Helga, her throat cut from ear to ear.

Item. Regina had been carrying on an affair with Will Foley.

Item. Helga had had a less-torrid affair with Will last summer.

Item. Will Foley was incarcerated when Regina was brutally murdered.

"Drop it," Gerald advised Quarles.

"Maybe. Maybe not."

Well, why rub it in? Quarles was no idiot. He saw that he would be wasting county money prosecuting Foley, to say nothing of exposing himself to defeat.

Susannah buzzed to say that Rebecca Prell was in the outer office and wished to see him.

"Send her in," Gerald cried expansively. Doubtless the reporter wanted him to draw out the implications of the Regina Foote murder for the case against his client, Will Foley. Gerald was more than willing to lecture the potential jury pool via the public press on what this second murder meant with respect to the innocence of Will Foley. But Rebecca brushed all triumphalism aside.

"I think I know who did it."

She spoke intensely. Gerald was deflated by the ease with which she consigned the Will Foley case to the ash can of history. Her interest was focused on the far more important point of who had killed these two women.

"Who do you think did it?"

His tone gave her pause. She dipped her chin and looked across the desk at him. "Maybe I shouldn't bother you with this."

She was cute as button, Rebecca Prell, the polar opposite of the regal Julie. Rebecca belonged on a tennis court, in a rowing shell, rock climbing. He imagined her in shorts and a tailored shirt, a sweatband adding a native touch to her well-scrubbed wholesome beauty. Today she wore a white dress with huge blue polka dots. It would have been all wrong for Julie, but it was perfect on Rebecca.

"Nice dress."

"Thanks."

"I liked the yellow one too."

Was that a blush on the cheeks of the ambitious no-nonsense reporter for the *Dealer*? Even apart from the impediment of Julie, Gerald would have hesitated about asking Rebecca out. She was like the little sister of a lifelong friend, or a distant cousin, someone you could like only up to a point without transgressing some taboo.

"Where'd you get that tie?"

"Don't you like it?"

She stuck a finger in her mouth and simulated gagging. The tie was a gift from Julie, bought in the gift shop of the Marriott a few days before as a memento of their flying trip to Schaumberg.

"So who killed those two women?"

"You were in the Rancho Rango last night."

"How did you know that?"

"I'm a reporter."

"Were you there?"

"The important thing is that Regina Foote was there. If you had danced you might have noticed her."

"But I wouldn't have known her."

"I said you would have noticed her, not that you knew her. She was very conspicuous. She was there with Charlie Hughes."

Gerald had tucked his tie in and buttoned his jacket. He was waiting for her to say more.

"Charlie is the brother of Mrs. Foley. Fiona."

"Is that how you pronounce it?"

"That's the way she does."

"So her brother was with the woman who was found dead this morning." He frowned and reached for the paper. He found what he was looking for. "The body was discovered by Charlie Hughes."

"That's right."

"You think he killed her."

"It's just a theory."

"Go ahead."

But she hesitated. What had brought her bounding to the offices of Andrew Broom appeared to be less convincing to her now. Why shouldn't she suspect the man who had been with the slain woman and also reported her dead the following morning? He nodded as she spoke, from time to time taking notes.

"Better tell Quarles."

"Would you?"

"Why not you?"

"I'm a reporter. I'm not supposed to be part of the story."

"Well, you can't very well be neutral when two young women have their throats cut."

She winced at this reference to the method of killing. He told her he would call Quarles and pass on what she had told him.

"You ever play tennis?"

"When I'm asked."

He laughed. "How about today?"

"Where?"

He hesitated. "Indoor or outdoor?"

"Don't you belong to the country club?"

He could hardly tell her that he ran the risk of being seen there by Julie McGough. Maybe he could tell Julie he was being interviewed.

"We can continue this conversation there."

"Don't you want to call the sheriff first?"

"Of course."

The murder of Regina Foote blew Andrew's theory out of the water, but Gerald did not make that point while he told him that there was good reason to think that Charlie Hughes was the killer.

"He was out with her the night she was killed."

"Didn't he claim to have found the body too?"

"He also had an interest in Helga."

The center of gravity of these events moved back toward those around Will Foley. Even so, Andrew was reluctant to give up on the fusion of the two cases, the heirs of Stanley Waggoner and the bodies found in Will Foley's car. The attempt on Sonny Apple, the two deaths of other people on the list of bloodline heirs, along with that of Helga, had suggested looking for the one who was increasing his slice of the pie by lessening the numbers of those at the table. And Jeb Riverside was cunning and greedy enough to fill that role. Emil was on the job, keeping a watch on Riverside, and Andrew would keep him on it for a while no matter what.

Of course, he had poured over the names on that list, wondering if Regina Foote could possibly be among the heirs. But there was no female below the age of forty-five remaining.

"No one but the mailman," Cleary replied when Andrew asked if there had been anyone around Mrs. Bjornsen's house.

"No prowlers?"

"Andrew, as far as we know, the only prowlers she actually saw were you and Gerald."

"You think she was imagining it?"

"Some day I'll tell you about my Aunt Eunice."

"I look forward to it."

Emil had nothing significant to report the first two days he had Jeb Riverside under surveillance. Andrew asked himself what he expected to happen. He had told Emil to go where Jeb went, so if he made a trip to Schaumberg, Emil would follow along and report whatever he did.

One thing that heartened Andrew was the interest that Gerald was taking in the reporter from the *Dealer*, Rebecca Prell. They had played tennis at the club, he had taken her to lunch at Luigi's, he asked her along when he and Andrew were scheduled to play golf.

"So much for you know who," Andrew whispered elatedly to Susannah.

"Julie? I believe she's out of town."

Even so, while the cat was away . . .

Rebecca played tennis better than she golfed, to put it charitably, and Andrew repressed thoughts of the lithe and rhythmic Julie sending her drives well out into the fairway. There was nothing fundamentally wrong with Rebecca's game, she simply did not have confidence in her ability. What had to become automatic was still calculated and thought out.

"That will come," he assured her.

"You might have warned me that you two are practically pros," she said to Gerald.

Afterward they had drinks on the terrace and Andrew floated an idea that he thought might step things up and force someone to make a move. It was an idea he should have generalized as soon as he realized that Mrs. Bjornsen would now fall heir to the money meant for Helga. But this was true of all now departed members of the bloodline heirs. He suggested it to Rebecca as a human interest story.

"The original list is fascinating in itself. And the magnanimity with which Stanley Waggoner accepted the claims as soon as he saw they were based on genuine consanguinity is noteworthy. Of course, he owed them nothing. One does not have an obligation to leave money to relatives, though they can make claim to it in the absence of a will."

"Could you get me a copy of the list?"

"Gerald would be happy to do that." He smiled benevolently, as if blessing their possible union.

"Helga Bjornsen was on that list," Gerald pointed out.

"She was? Why?"

"It's a list of people with Waggoner blood in their veins."

"But she was adopted." Clearly this was a spoor Rebecca

felt far more inclination to pursue than the generic human interest story Andrew had suggested the whole list involved.

"The money will now go to her mother."

"But she can't have Waggoner blood, can she?"

"She is the heir of her daughter and need not fulfill the conditions Helga had to in order to make that list. That can be said of anyone who died before the will was probated."

"Has anyone died?"

"How many is it, Gerald, two or three?"

Thus he passed the ball to Gerald, who now saw the drift of Andrew's suggestion; Andrew presumed that he could influence the direction Rebecca's interest in the Waggoner will took.

"If the same man who killed Helga killed Regina Foote, there isn't much of a connection, is there? With the heirs, I mean."

"Not an obvious one," Andrew said, avoiding Gerald's eyes. He wondered if he had become that most foolish of mortals, a man in the grips of a theory.

Rebecca found Gerald's sudden interest in her exhilarating, but at the same time she did not quite believe it. He was fun to be with, particularly when they played tennis, and it was nice to have someone more mentally prepossessing than Emil Broadbeck to squire her about, although she had the sense that pressure was being subtly applied to her. Still, she was already inclined to do a follow-up story on Helga. The fact that the slain girl had been in line to inherit money from the Waggoner estate added poignancy to her death.

"That her mother now gets the money is a nice angle too," Gerald said.

"Do you think that's why there were prowlers around her house?" Rebecca asked.

"If there were."

"Prowlers could mean that the wrong people have already drawn the conclusion that the inheritance can be passed on to next of kin."

Gerald looked at her. Of course she was right. He and Andrew had come to the conclusion that Mrs. Bjornsen's prowlers had been imaginary. To satisfy himself, Cleary had Hanson look around the place to see if there was any evidence of prowlers and Hanson had turned up nothing conclusive.

"Then there weren't any?"

"I didn't say that. I said I find no evidence there were any."

"Doesn't that come down to the same thing?"

"Not in logic."

Hanson could be a tough guy to deal with, particularly when he decided to get on his high horse—well, medium-sized horse—and treat every question as if it were out of order.

"I'm going to pull the deputy off that duty."

Hanson had no comment on that and Cleary realized he was waiting for one. That made him angry with himself. He was not asking Hanson's permission, for crying out loud. He had looked at Gerald with an expression Gerald now tried to convey to Rebecca.

"Have you ever thought of writing?"

"To whom?"

She laughed. He was really fun, but she knew he belonged to Julie. She became convinced of this when her rival came up in a conversation with Andrew Broom. Andrew had said how much he enjoyed seeing her with Gerald. He complimented her on her tennis game. He suggested golf lessons to bring her golf into the same league as her tennis.

"Does Julie play tennis?" Rebecca asked, surprising herself by the question.

"Julie?"

"Julie McGough."

"What does she have to do with this conversation?"

"Someone told me she had a proprietary interest in Gerald."

He tried to laugh, but it obviously hurt too much. "That's not true." He hesitated. "Of course, it would be gauche for me to say that you have an open track."

"They're not engaged?"

"Over my dead body. And her father feels the same way."

He never did regain his aplomb after that and Rebecca came away convinced that all she could expect from Gerald was the pleasure of his company. Competing with Julie McGough would be like going up against Miss America.

Driving downtown, she stopped at a light and the horn of the car that pulled up beside her blasted. She turned warily and there was the grinning face of Emil Broadbeck. She rolled down her window and he shouted, "Pull in at McDonald's. We'll have coffee."

Rebecca agreed although she was afloat in coffee after her talk with Andrew Broom. Emil loped across the lot to her and for a mad moment Rebecca thought he would sweep her into his arms. Before she could figure out what she would think of that, he had her by the elbow and was steering her toward the entrance.

"Let's get out of this heat."

Was it warm? It was cold enough inside. So much for her thought that she would throw caution to the winds and have a chocolate shake. Nothing cold would welcome in the air-conditioned frigidity of the franchise food place. Emil's knees bumped into hers beneath the table, but it was accidental. He still had the infectious grin he had directed from his car to hers.

"What a stroke of luck to run into you just when I have a minute."

"You're that busy?"

He looked over both shoulders. "I finally figured out the nature of my assignment."

"But you can't tell me?"

"Sure I can. But you can't tell anyone else."

She neither agreed nor disagreed, but it didn't matter. He was dying to talk about what he had been doing. It sounded like a definition of boredom to Rebecca, keeping out of sight while he never let Jeb Riverside out of his.

"Jeb Riverside?"

Emil inhaled. "What do you know of the Waggoner will?"

"Tell me."

He had it somewhat garbled. He thought that it was some kind of contest between Catherine Waggoner and the claimants, winner take all. But that wasn't where the real action was.

"That list has shrunk over the past half year."

"Shrunk?"

"A violent death, a mysterious accident. A car rigged to come unglued in traffic." His eyes held hers in an almost hypnotic gaze. "Right after Jeb Riverside paid him a visit."

"Ah."

"And of course there is Helga Bjornsen."

"You think Jeb Riverside had something to do with those deaths?"

"The important thing is that Andrew Broom thinks so. That's why he hired me."

"Who's watching Jeb Riverside now?"

"My father." He glanced at his watch. "I was on my way home to catch a few hours' sleep."

"What if something happens while you're not there?"

Emil unhooked a pager from his belt and showed it to her. "If my dad wants to get in touch he can beep me."

Even as he said this the device began to beep. People turned to see what the noise was. "I must have hit something," Emil said, beginning to redden. "I'll turn it off."

But it continued beeping. The attention of everyone in the restaurant was on Emil, who could not stop the pager.

"Maybe's it's your father, Emil."

He bounded from his chair and down a little hallway to a public phone, taking the beeping sound with him. Eventually it stopped. Then Emil came running back to the table, a look of astonishment on his face.

"It *was* Dad. I've got to go."

He looked around at the other diners as if he would have liked to tell them the disturbance had been no accident, some-one was trying to reach him.

"Keep in touch, Emil."

He turned to go, then stopped and came back. "When this assignment is over . . ."

She nodded and put her hand on his. "Of course."

Rebecca was surprised that Andrew Broom was investing so much time in the theory that the killing of two Wyler women was somehow connected to the heirs of Stanley Waggoner, particularly after the death of Regina Foote. Emil's dogged dutifulness about his assignment made her want to hold him. Just hold him. How could she tell him he was on a fool's errand.

206

A note on her desk told her that Gladys Winter had called. She dialed the number given and listened to the ringing go on and on. It occurred to her that Gladys could cast light on the relationship between Regina and Charlie Hughes.

Hanson was edgy because the pornography theory of the death of Helga Bjornsen had been overcome by events. Neither Cleary nor any of his deputies had said anything, but it was Andrew Broom's reminder of the skin flick account that Hanson dreaded. It was not rare for a cop to become obsessed with the crimes and evils he was sworn to fight. In large cities, at least, there were men who had dual employment in the police department and in organized crime. Men on the vice squad often developed an unsavory interest in vice. It was the accusation that he was hung up on pornography that Hanson feared. Because there was some truth in it.

He had played the evidence he had gathered in Bloomington on the VCR in his motel room in Wyler and he would have had to be a man of steel to be unaffected by it. It was the beauty and seeming innocence of the girls who romped upon the screen that was the most corrupting thing about such videos. How easy to think that any girl one passed on the street was eager to cavort like those in the film.

He rinsed his mind free of the images and turned to the fact that the murder of Regina Foote looked like Will Foley's ticket out of jail.

As with the first girl, Helga, the woman had been killed in the car in which she was found, in the same car, as it happened. There was something absurd in this, as if someone were trying to implicate Foley just when there was no way in which he could have been involved.

Hanson called Regina's husband, Dr. Foote the podiatrist, at the used car lot where he worked part-time until he got his practice built up. They arranged to meet at the doctor's office.

There was a large plastic foot on his desk that could be opened up to show patients the inner workings of their pedal extremities. "Go ahead and laugh. Not only is my name Foote, I married a Bunyan."

"I'm surprised you're seeing patients again so soon." The waiting room had been empty and the receptionist looked as if she had slipped in for the occasion.

"You called me. Who are you exactly?"

Hanson took out his identification, slowly, looking at Foote as he did so, then laid it on the desk.

"I didn't know there was an Indiana Bureau of Investigation."

"There is."

"What can I do for you?"

Behind the desk there was a door and Hanson was thinking how easily Foote could slip away and that would mean going in pursuit of him. With the way his sciatica was acting up that was not a welcome prospect. It was hard to tell if Foote was the running type. Cleary had already talked with Foote.

"He was very cooperative," Cleary reported.

Hanson had read the record of those conversations. Foote claimed to know nothing of his wife's night life and extramarital affairs. Hanson brought that up now.

"Long leash, long marriage, ever hear that?"

"No, I hadn't. You don't care what your wife did?"

"I didn't say that. But as long as she's discreet . . ."

Hanson could imagine a woman saying this, but a man? He did not believe that Foote regarded his wife's infidelity casually, even if he himself were not the best of husbands. The double standard was still in effect in the hearts of most men and Foote did not look like a man who had risen above it and was willing to accord women the same liberty in sexual matters as some men claimed. Was Foote one of those men? The quickest way to find out was to ask him.

"You writing a book or investigating my wife's murder?"

"Who would want to murder her?"

"Not me."

"Some other man?"

His shoulders and brows lifted. "She complained about Will Foley."

"Will Foley was in jail when she was killed."

"That's where I would want to be if I hired someone to kill for me."

"Who would kill for Will Foley?"

"Hey, you're the detective, not me."

"Are you making an accusation?"

Foote brought both hands to his chest as if seeking an accordion keyboard. "Me?" Then he leaned forward, serious. "But I want the son of a bitch who killed Regina to pay for it."

"He will," Hanson promised with a bravura he did not feel. "Who were your wife's friends?"

"Friends?"

"Women friends."

"Oh." He thought about it. "A girl named Gladys Winter, for one."

Will Foley was profusive in his thanks when they emerged from the courthouse and the cemetery maintenance man once more breathed free air. Andrew told him that it was Gerald he should thank.

"And whoever killed Regina Foote."

Foley was unknotting his tie with one hand and using the other to squirm out of his sport jacket, clothes he had been urged to wear in court and now shed as the final proof of his release. Andrew shook his hand and watched Foley, jacket thrown over his shoulder, skip down the steps to a red pickup waiting at the curb. Because of the tinted glass it was difficult to tell who was at the wheel.

"Charlie Hughes," Gerald said.

"How's Hanson progressing with that?"

Gerald didn't know, but why should he? His energy had been focused on getting the charges against Foley dropped and their client out of jail on the basis of the Regina Foote slaying.

"Both dead women had affairs with Will Foley."

"Maybe Fiona Foley did away with them."

The implausibility of this seemed obvious on the face of it. Foley's wife was passive under the blows of life. Her husband was her fate, her children were her cross, her house was her place in this vale of tears. Her loyalty had the intensity of one for whom this life held no promise at all.

"It's about as likely as that she would have killed her husband."

"So?"

This conversation continued in a booth in the Round Ball Lounge, off the Lobby of the Hoosier Towers. "So we need someone who knew the two women and their relation to Foley."

"And who resented it."

"Right. Fiona Foley is out. Cleary checked her whereabouts on the nights of both slayings, just to make absolutely sure. She's out of the picture."

"Regina's husband?"

Hanson wrinkled his nose. "It's possible, but unattractive."

"How so?"

"Possible only with respect to his wife. There is no way to link him to Helga Bjornsen's death."

"It violates the principle of parsimony? One suspect is better than two."

"The deaths are connected."

"Through Foley?"

Hanson nodded. "Through Foley."

"So who's your link?"

"Charlie Hughes."

Andrew and Gerald exchanged a glance. "He picked Foley up at the courthouse just now," Gerald said. "He came to see him in jail. They're friends."

"He has the motive Fiona would have if she were a different person."

"His sister's honor?"

Hanson picked up his glass, then returned it to the table without drinking. "The problem is what you said. Charlie has been a friend, even a fan, of Foley's since they were kids. His solitary boast has been that Will Foley married his sister."

"Forget Fiona. Say Charlie is a fanatically devoted friend. Say Foley did indeed kill Helga. What got Foley out of the slammer was the death of Regina. Charlie could have killed her as a big favor to his old buddy."

"He was out dancing with Regina the night she was killed."

Gerald said, "Hughes sounds like your man."

42

Gladys Winter was already at the office when she heard the news of the murder of Regina and her first reaction was to lock herself in the bathroom and just stare at herself in the mirror over the sink. It was like the morning that Helga's body had been found in the car parked there at the cemetery. Gladys was filled with the irrational certainty that she herself was next.

Her hand went to her throat and she cried aloud. The bathroom had seemed a refuge, but now she felt trapped. She unlocked the door and opened it hardly at all, just enough to slip out. She hurried across the room to the door of the inner office and stepped into the darkened room. She pressed her forehead against the frame of the door, aware of her own breathing, aware of the beating of her heart. She did not want to hear her heart beat. She did not want to be reminded what a fragile hold she had on life. The rhythmic pulse went on and on; it had been going on since she was an infant, but one day it would stop, either because her heart just wore out or because someone did to her what had been done to Helga and Regina.

There was a sound behind her in the darkened room and the beat of her heart was suddenly more audible. Her hands still gripped the doorknob; it would be so easy just to pull the door open and step into her own bright office, but she felt frozen in place.

"Is something the matter?"

She turned. Junius Schmucker, his face illumined by his monitor, reflecting the flickering screen he faced, stared at her as if he had just risen from the grave. That is what she would have seen under ordinary circumstances. But these were not ordinary circumstances. What she saw was an apparition, a visitation by the devil. She let out a shriek and began to tug at the door, but it would not open. When the hand closed on her wrist, she sank screaming to the floor.

"Gladys," the voice insistently said, "Gladys, for God's sake, shut up. You're all right. There's nothing to worry about."

She opened her eyes and became aware of the upside-down moon face of Junius Schmucker. The noise she heard was her own screaming that seemed to have a mind of its own. It stopped because he clamped a hand over her mouth. She was almost grateful. But then the door to her office opened. Charlie Hughes stood there.

"What in hell are you doing, Schmucker?"

"She was hysterical," Junius cried, his voice trembling.

"No wonder." Charlie flicked a switch and flooded the room

with light. Junius edged away, moving toward the back door.

"Regina has been murdered, Charlie," Gladys cried.

"That's what she's been screaming," Junius said.

"First Helga, now Regina."

Charlie nodded his head. The back door closed on Junius's exit. Gladys realized that she had collapsed into an unladylike position, and she began to tug at her skirt to get it down somewhere in the neighborhood of her knees. She twisted around, tugging, and, looking up, saw that Charlie's eyes were on her knees. Minutes ago she had been in terror of her life, now she took a vague pride in the fact that a man was noticing that she had very attractive limbs. Her legs were the best thing about her, and it was her cross that she could not wear shorts to work in the summer. Not only would it have been too informal, it was cold as ice in the air-conditioned office, even colder in Junius's. He perspired easily and required near-Arctic air to control his ducts and pores. Charlie, it dawned on Gladys, was one of the few unmarried men she knew. He helped her to her feet.

"All right now?"

"Thank you."

"You're shivering."

"It's so cold in here."

"You ought to get out in the sun."

"I'd like to drive to the dunes and just lie on the sand."

"I'll take you there."

"Are you serious?"

"I think you need some time away from here. You were very distraught."

Distraught. She liked the word. Charlie was in his way an educated man. Had she ever been called distraught before?

They slipped out the back way and into his car with the tinted windows and within minutes were rolling north toward Lake Michigan and the dunes along its southern shore. The car had a CD player and Charlie put on some New Age music.

"I don't have a bathing suit," she said.

"What?" He seemed not to have heard.

"Nothing."

This was spontaneous, unplanned. Of course she didn't have a bathing suit. She felt reckless and carefree. Regina should see me, she thought, and then remembered. But she refused to think about it. She drove all the awful thoughts from her mind and smiled vacantly ahead, toward sand and sun and an absence of thought.

When the fat sexton came out of the building and got into his Lincoln Town Car, Hanson sat immobile behind the wheel of his rented car. But the man was too preoccupied to notice Hanson's car. Hughes was still inside. Hanson had spotted the red truck emerging from the Foley driveway and followed it, wondering how best to handle Hughes. On the one hand, the guy seemed a wimp. On the other, he might have murdered two women in cold blood.

Hanson froze when the door opened and the woman Gladys came out. Hughes followed, closing the door behind him and looking around before dancing down the steps and opening the passenger door for Gladys. Come into my parlor, said the spider to the fly.

Hanson let them get a start and then set off after them. He had the feeling he was about to be there for Act Three of Charlie Hughes's bloody drama.

43

Rebecca smiled at the image of Emil's awkward effort in the restaurant to stop the pager that indicated his father wanted him to call. As he explained it, he kept his vigil at a distance, parked on a dirt road that ran behind a golfing range. From there he must have a pretty bleak view of the backs of the signs marking distances from the tee. She wondered if she would be able to visit Jeb Riverside without being watched by Emil.

She pulled off the highway into the lot of the driving range, parking behind a car so that Emil would not pick her out from his vigil three hundred yards away.

Rebecca slid across the seat and got out on the passenger side, with the building between her and Emil. Inside it was cool and musty and smelled of leather and oil and plastic. On the counter were two wire buckets of different sizes filled with golf balls with red stripes painted around them.

"Club provided," said the large man behind the counter.

"I'm Rebecca Prell of the *Dealer* and I just turned in on the spur of the moment. Is there a story here? That's what I asked myself. Are you Lefty?"

"Lefty's lying in his last divot."

"He's dead?"

"But immortalized in the name of the business he created." He handed her a little brochure. On the front was a very idealized picture of the range; inside, a narrative linked the site of the range with the history of the area.

"You inherited it?"

"Lefty was my uncle, but no, I bought the business from his widow."

"And you're Jeb Riverside?" The name was on the little brochure.

"Proprietor and general manager."

"I recognize the name."

"Recognize it?"

"From the list of heirs of Stanley Waggoner."

She had surprised him. "The will hasn't been probated yet. How could you know that?"

"I'm a reporter. People tell me things."

Jeb smiled at her in a humorless way. "Well, I'm not one of them."

He came around the counter, glowering, and indicated that she should leave. He came outside with her and closed the door of the shop. Without taking any further notice of her, he shambled off to the ball-retrieving tractor and started the motor, causing an enormous unmuffled racket and a cloud of black smoke. Then he was bouncing off onto the range dragging the large device that picked up the balls. Rebecca sat on a wooden bench under the eave of the shack and watched Riverside go methodically back and forth, picking up the balls that had been hit out at varying distances by his customers. At the moment there were no golfers on the rubber mat hitting red-striped balls into the distance.

The bench she sat on was grooved with age; initials and names had been whittled into it but were smoothed now with time. It was possible to believe that the driving range was exactly as it had been when the eponymous Lefty ran it. Rebecca watched the man on the tractor, the long bill of his cap shading his face, his body bouncing as the tractor responded to the uneven contours of the range. Was Riverside soon to come into money that would enable him to look back with amusement on these days when he waited for passersby to be struck with the impulse to hit a bucket of balls?

She picked up a dog-eared magazine from the bench and almost immediately put it down again. This was a guys' place, obviously. She belatedly realized that she would be visible to Emil three hundred yards away on the far side of the range. She shaded her eyes and sought his car but objects in the distance became hazy in the heat. A stick figure stood beside a vehicle and Rebecca saw a little puff and then after an interval heard a distant report. This was repeated, and then she saw that Riverside had begun to maneuver the tractor. He had turned toward the shack and was zigzagging in her direction, his mouth open. He was yelling, but whatever he was shouting was drowned out by the tractor's motor.

Off in the distance, hazy, almost imaginary, the stick figure continued to shoot at Jeb Riverside.

44

Emil took the glasses away from his eyes, blinked, and then looked again. The girl who had come out of the range shack door with Riverside sure looked like Rebecca. Jeb walked away from her and went to his tractor, but Emil kept the glasses on Rebecca.

Sitting there by the hour, watching a jerk like Riverside, made a man wonder if some jobs were worth doing. If he were working for anyone other than Andrew Broom he would have cashed in after two days of this kind of duty. Boredom took on new dimensions as he sat there hour after hour. Customers took up their stance from time to time and hit balls more or less in Emil's direction. Most of them seemed to be practicing how to be bad. Emil was almost elated when he did get a good look at Riverside. Of course, there was the constant worry that the guy would slip away, leaving Emil there watching a deserted driving range. But he had a fix on Jeb's car and any time that moved he would.

Now he left the glasses on Rebecca. He remembered their line dancing, he remembered holding her in his arms at the movies. Everything was perfect between them as long as he didn't have to talk. He would notice her eyes glaze over when he talked about golf, but the fact was that golf was the one thing he knew about. The big question was whether he could make it as a professional golfer. This job represented his best chance since he had believed the line of bull Jeb Riverside had given him a year before. But Andrew Broom would deliver.

The previous afternoon, dead tired from doing nothing all day, he had gone home by way of the country club and hit a pail of seemingly brand-new balls. The range had the look of a regular hole; to practice there was to get ready for the real thing. As soon as Jeb Riverside did whatever it was Andrew expected him to do, Emil would devote himself to intensive preparation for competition. In his mind's eye he could already see the trophies he would win, starting small and moving up, step by step to . . .

He shook the thought away. He was getting groggy but he did not want to ask his dad to spell him. The other day he had come dashing back in response to his father's beeper only to find that his father wanted to know how in hell to turn the thing off.

"You weren't sending for me?"

"Of course I was. How long is the damned thing going to make noise?"

Emil took the beeper and pressed the battery pack latch and disengaged one of the AAs. That shut it off.

"I'll take over, Dad."

"But you need rest."

"I just needed a break. I feel okay."

It didn't take much convincing. Emil clapped his dad on the shoulder and sent him on his way. He had been remembering that when he saw Rebecca come out the door with Jeb Riverside.

What made her tick? She threw herself into her work, she was good at it, but it did not seem to give her much satisfaction. When she talked about Ross Pigot, Emil didn't like it. The guy obviously grated on her. He did easily what she did with effort and he didn't care. There were golfers like that . . .

The sound fifty yards to his left might have been anything, but when it was repeated again and again, there was no doubt it was gunfire. A guy was standing next to the hood of his car, holding a rifle and blasting away at Jeb Riverside on the tractor. Jeb had veered off course and was now making for the shelter of the shack, zigzagging as he went. It probably was only a matter of seconds, but Emil had the sense that he was just standing there with his mouth open, looking back and forth from the rifleman to Jeb. And then he was sprinting toward the man with the rifle.

He was almost on him when the man lowered the rifle and released the empty clip. He was digging in his pocket when he turned and saw Emil coming at him. Panic. But then he had another clip out of his pocket and was trying to jam it into the rifle, half doubled over as he did, his eyes never leaving Emil. Emil went for him, right over the hood of the car, just taking off as if he were going into a pool. He hit the rifleman just as he turned away and the force of the impact took them both to the ground. Emil saw the new clip bounce along the ground so he wasn't worried about the rifle anymore.

Even so he ripped it from the man's hands, straddled his body and was about to punch him out when he realized the guy was damned near sixty years old and panting as if he were going to have a heart attack. Emil was puffing a bit himself. And then he heard the sound of the siren. The man he had pinned listened to it as attentively as Emil, as if that is what they had both been waiting for.

Coming toward him across the driving range, her arms and legs going like crazy, was Rebecca. Jeb Riverside kept going toward the office, so he must be all right. Sitting astride the panting old man the age of his dad, Emil watched Rebecca running to him. He picked up the beeper then and hit the numbers that would alert Andrew Broom.

45

The rifleman was Mark Larson and he might have been mute for all that Cleary and his deputy Dwayne Streeter could get out of him. Why had he been taking potshots at Jeb Riverside? That Larson had intended mortal harm to Riverside was clear from the wounds that the driving range operator had sustained. A bullet had gone through his knee, another had grazed his skull and a third had passed within millimeters of his lungs before it emerged from his chest. That one might have been the coup de grace. Jeb was rushed to the hospital, where he was listed as critical for the first twenty-four hours of his stay.

"Who the hell was he?" were his first words when he emerged from the sedative.

"His name is Larson."

Riverside looked confused. "The old duffer who hung around the range?"

"Is he on the list?" Gerald asked him.

Riverside did not need to be told which list. "No."

But it was Andrew who remembered Darlene Bjornsen's ill-starred marriage to a man named Larson. Apparently it had never been legally dissolved. Larson could lay claim to the money that came his wife's way from what had been left to Helga. He knew more about the provisions Stanley Waggoner had made than his erstwhile wife, but then he had spent hours listening to Jeb Riverside babble about his prospects. Jeb's remark about the advantages of fewer slices of pie had impressed him. He had systematically set about lessening the number of blood claimaints to the Waggoner fortune.

Larson actually perked up when the accusation was made, ticking off his victims and near victims with the pride of a craftsman. That his exploits excited the grudging admiration of his accusers loosened his lips.

He had been the driver of the hit-and-run car in Detroit, he had strangled the woman in Milwaukee, he had worked on Sonny Apple's car, and when he failed to bring about a fatal accident, he had set fire to Sonny's condo, unaware that Sonny had taken refuge across the creek with Cynthia Thanos.

"But your own wife and daughter," Andrew said.

"Wife! What kind of wife was she? And don't talk to me abut her daughter. That was her daughter, not mine."

"If Helga hadn't had the father she had, there wouldn't have been the money you've done all this killing trying to get."

But Larson was impervious to irony. All that killing. And of course, turning Jeb Riverside's golfing range into a shooting gallery. Riverside was surprised to hear that it had been Emil who had saved his life. If Larson had gotten a fresh clip into his rifle, he would very likely have put several more rounds into the fleeing Riverside.

"He's still a son of a bitch," Emil said when interviewed on the tenth tee at the country club. He was playing thirty-six holes a day and his game had improved dramatically. "I imagine Jeb Riverside out there in his tractor and drill the ball to that point."

"Something like that," Andrew said when Emil asked him if it was the attack on Jeb by the rifleman that he had been hired to witness.

There remained, of course, the element of Regina Foote's murder. Hanson's bruised eye was a reminder he could have done without. He had got it when he snuck up on the presumed Bluebeard Charlie Hughes when Hughes disappeared under a blanket with Gladys Winter. The IBI agent had seen what appeared to be the sparkle of a steel blade before the blanket closed over them and he moved as quickly as he could through the sand, wanting to stop to take off his shoes but not daring to spare the time. He stumbled just short of the blanket but reached out and grabbed a corner, yanking it off. The result was the exposure of a scene not unlike that featured in the videos Hanson had been studying of late. He sat back in the sand, amazed.

"I'm sorry," he began. But the enraged Hughes, swaddled in a towel, swung at him with the first nonfleshy thing he could lay his hands on, a portable Geiger counter, and then began to pummel the hapless agent while a now-decent Gladys looked smugly on.

*   *   *

"At least it wasn't a blood relative of Stanley's," Catherine Drexel Waggoner said after she had listened to the complicated account of what Darlene Bjornsen's all-but-forgotten husband had been up to.

"Once removed and by marriage," Susannah said obscurely.

"And in the end he intended to kill his wife as well?"

"He had been skulking around her house."

Catherine had come unexpectedly to the office and Susannah was entertaining her until Andrew returned from the court-house. Frank McGough had produced another nurse from the rest home where Stanley Waggoner had spent his last days. The nurse, Philip Church, was prepared to testify that Catherine had used every wile and subtle pressure to worm her way into the confidence and then affection of the aged Stanley.

Catherine laughed. "Stanley chided him about the earring he wore and Philip never forgave him."

"His testimony can hardly outweigh the fact of the will and the testimony of Father Campbell."

That matters could be that simple was not what readers of the *Dealer* had been led to think. Foster was obviously determined to handle the dispute between the town's two leading lawyers in the most evenhanded way possible. Columns were devoted to an interview Rebecca had conducted with Philip Church over the phone. The male nurse came through as the protector of honor and honesty.

"I know what I'm going to do," Catherine said.

"What?"

"I am going to relinquish all claim to any of Stanley's money."

Susannah looked at her. "Catherine, he wanted you to have it."

"But I never wanted it. I told him that. I never understood how much there was or all the trouble it would cause."

"This isn't trouble," Susannah urged. "It is a tempest in a teapot. No one will be swayed by what Philip Church says."

Catherine repositioned her hands in her lap and sat smiling. Clearly her mind was made up. Susannah felt a sense of vertigo at the spectacle of someone dismissing a fortune with the wave of a hand. But she felt admiration too. Catherine was able-bodied and attractive, so she could go on supporting herself; perhaps a less-unusual match awaited her in the future. That simple prospect must have seemed particularly attractive now that she had been caught up in a public dispute about her behavior in becoming Stanley's wife. But it was the fact that Larson had been willing to kill a number of fellow human beings in order to enlarge the sum of money he hoped to lay claim to after he killed Darlene Bjornsen that made the thought of being an heiress distasteful to Catherine.

"I can't let you do that," Andrew said when Catherine told him what she had decided.

"Right now I would rather enter a convent than inherit all that money."

Andrew looked to Susannah for help. It was startling enough that Catherine spoke of turning her back on millions but to suggest that she might disappear into a cloister was far beyond anything that Andrew could understand. He sat, waiting for his wife to address this new twist in Catherine's reaction to the turmoil Frank McGough was stirring up about the Waggoner inheritance.

"Why don't we just let things stand for a few days. You

could go home and get away from all this hullabaloo. That would give you time to think of all the good you can do with that money. I know you'll want to help Father Campbell."

This was just the reminder that Catherine needed. Not that she was persuaded. She was still in the grips of the attraction of just stepping out of the role Stanley had cast her in and leaving others to fight and quarrel over the money he had left behind.

It was while Catherine was rusticating and Andrew was preparing for the battle with Frank McGough over the will of Stanley Waggoner that the final piece fell into place. Quarles was salivating at the prospect of prosecuting Larson but Cleary was still faced with the need to investigate the death of Regina Foote. Hanson had gone back to Indianapolis, taking with him the bottle of sand from the Indiana dunes that Andrew gave him as a souvenir. Gerald had persuaded Hughes, using Foley as intermediary, to put aside thoughts of bringing charges against Hanson as a deviant voyeur who was a menace to lovers on the beach.

"It would embarrass Gladys, Charlie."

"She's the one pushing it."

"She'd probably lose her job at Overlook."

This thought gave revenge a worthy rival. Charlie clearly did not like the idea of a wife without an income.

"But who killed Regina?" Gladys asked.

It was Rebecca who turned up the final clue. Ross Pigot, her nemesis, had proposed doing a series of essays on the recent victims of violence in the community.

"I'm working on that," Rebecca said.

Foster was surprised. "I didn't realize that."

Piggie seemed almost relieved as the prospect of work faded. But then Rebecca was stuck with the task of dreaming up a series that would rival any Piggie might have produced, no simple matter. It was when she was pouring over Regina Foote's obituary that the light went on. Regina Bunyan Foote. Bunyan. Bunyan. She started a search on her computer and came upon the name Bunyan in another obituary, that of Leonard Bunyan, who had died some thirty years before. He was the father of Regina and the son of the deceased Eleanor Bunyan. Eleanor in turn was the sister of Stanley Waggoner!

Rebecca brought the news in person to Gerald Rowan, who took her by the hand and led her in to see Andrew. The senior partner had been engrossed in his work, but at the news he sprang to his feet and took Rebecca in his arms and kissed her ardently.

"Good girl!" He released her and turned her toward Gerald. It would have been ungallant not to follow suit. But Rebecca gave him only a cheek to kiss.

"But how did Larson know about that connection? Not even Riverside had learned of it."

"Larson is a patient of Dr. Foote's."

The two lawyers looked at the reporter. The podiatrist had added to the joke of his own name the fact that he had married a Bunyan. He would have used that quip with Larson, and Larson already knew of Eleanor Waggoner's married name.

"A unified theory," Andrew said with satisfaction.

Not quite I told you so. More an expression of relief.